KENTREE'S STOLEN SOULS

A Iles

Welcome to Kentree
Institute of Magic!

A Iles

Special thanks to the following people who were kind enough to donate their time to making Kentree's Stolen Souls the best it could be.

Diane Clement
Carmen Yolanda Perez Cadena
Steve Wendt
Brittany Olson
Judy Mulligan
and Doris Sawrie, who was the first to escape to Kentree.

CONTENTS

CHAPTER ONE
The Storm

Life was simply not magical enough for Eliza, who pulled into the driveway of her small one-bedroom bungalow. Eliza had chosen to purchase this as her first home some years before, moving away from the suburbs where she had been raised. She settled some forty-five minutes from her childhood home, in a small village where she could live a slower life. Far from the irritant air of daily traffic, she felt closer to nature and immediately fell in love with the charming village of Windham. Mature oak trees and birdsong had lined the streets that first time she visited, and it was just what she needed. Homeowners here were proud and kept their gardens neatly mown and their flower beds well fertilized.

While this village continued to charm Eliza years after her arrival, her garden drew some negative attention from her neighbours. It was now totally overgrown and taking over some of her house. Blackberry canes rested against the low sloping roof, their fruit ripening far out of reach of human hands. Coneflowers had gone to seed in the front yard, and the backyard contained a miniature meadow of un-tamed wildflowers. Eliza neglected to remove the dry stalks that remained, and black-eyed Susans, daisies, milkweed, and even dandelion heads were spilling their seeds onto the earth and into the air. There was a path, just wide enough for one person to tread carefully, that led from the driveway through the backyard toward a shed. Upon this path sat a small black cat, named Pal.

It was a fine September day; leaves had yet to turn, and wasps were feasting on fruit that had gone too long without being picked. Eliza slumped against her car in the driveway of her home and closed her eyes to breathe in the clean air. A woman from the village garden club had once told her that her garden had so much *potential*, that she could do so much with it. There had been a lot of gossip about the scandalous quantity of cotton-y milkweed seeds drifting away from Eliza's garden and into neighbouring properties. Windham villagers used phrases like, "Noxious weeds," to describe the flower that Monarch butterflies depend on for survival. One neighbour sourly glared at Eliza each time he stood with a backpack sprayer, dousing his lawn with herbicide wherever dandelions grew. How could she explain that the bright yellow flowers were food for bees (which often elicited a scandalized gasp from people afraid of a sting) and *beautiful* whether or not they were accused of being weeds?

Presently, though Eliza did not notice, a couple with a pram were crossing the street to avoid walking directly in front of her yard. The pavement in front of her house was strewn with overripe elderberries which would stain their nice white walking shoes. They exchanged glances with one another at seeing Eliza appearing to *admire* the disorder. The couple congratulated themselves for not being so bizarre and out-of-touch with presentability as Eliza.

The truth is, Eliza had perfected the garden to her needs. A fragrance of herbs and flowers drifted through the air, mixing with the earthy smell of decomposition. Perennial onions still stood firmly, bright green, among the many plants that were now going dormant in time for winter. Those onions would also be among the first plants to reappear in the spring when the snow melted, along with several hundred flowering Crocuses and Siberian Squills. Eliza could mix dozens of teas from the herbs and plants she grew, and with those she could cure most minor ailments (as long as those ailments were sore throats, headaches, and menstrual cramps).

Besides providing tea, food, and medicine for Eliza, it was also a place of refuge for many animals that had little where else to go. Though she lived in a village, the village was merely an island. It was surrounded by hundreds of acres of *productive* land. Agricultural fields that specialized in only two or three crops; mainly corn and soybeans. Eliza's overgrown garden provided the perfect hiding place for insects, birds, and mammals alike. Recently she became aware that there were other visitors to her garden, too. Visitors she could not see but whose presence was given away by certain clues. There was no denying it. A family of gnomes had made camp next to a toad's den, and the glittering pink and purple wings of faeries caught the evening light just before the fireflies began their own show. Yes, there was magic in this garden.

Eliza's day job left her feeling robotic and empty. She remembered being a teenager and being told she had her whole life ahead of her, anything was possible, she was brimming with potential. But life had only brought her to become an assistant in an office where she contributed nothing, created nothing, and aspired to nothing. Belonging in a society where it was more acceptable to spray poison on your grass, just meters from the well where you get your drinking water, than it was to let plants go to seed took its toll on Eliza. She often felt she'd been born in the wrong century, that the hubbub of normal life left much lacking in her soul.

Her garden was the only place that provided her

a sanctuary where she could fully believe that there was a world of magic and joy interconnected with the mundane one. A world of magic, faeries, and timeless eternal belonging. Here among the prickly canes of raspberry plants and stinging nettles, she could feel the turning of the seasons and the hum of something more than Ordinary singing beneath the surface of reality.

The grim expression she wore when she arrived from work was wiped away when the little black cat in the garden started to make its way toward her. Pal sauntered down the garden path, ducked beneath wild bergamot and hopped over flowering tufts of oregano and tarragon to arrive at Eliza's feet. She felt happiness with the arrival of the bouncing feline, whose tail was curved into the shape of an interrogation mark. Pal brushed himself heartily against Eliza's legs in welcome and she reached down and lifted him into her arms. He purred loudly while settling himself comfortably against her shoulder.

Eliza began to walk through the garden with Pal keeping a watchful eye out for birds and squirrels. She reached a patch of fragrant plants she had selected for their usefulness in herbal tea, and came to rest on her knees among them. Eliza released Pal from her embrace, and he bounded happily into a patch of red clover to catch a grasshopper. Running her hand along the tops of some herbs, a rich fragrance filled Eliza's senses.

All thought of her stressful workday were erased as the gentle smell of mint mixed with lemon and thyme swirled around her.

Laughter sprang from Eliza's lips when Pal dove headfirst into a gooseberry bush and all that was left of him were his hind legs poking ridiculously up in the air and his tail swirling wildly as he became tangled in the spiny branches. Eliza gently extracted the thrashing cat and stroked his head.

"Cats are supposed to be elegant, you know. And proud," teased Eliza.

"And humans aren't supposed to talk to cats," Pal retorted, tail twitching in embarrassment.

Eliza sighed, "It's a shame, in the old days they would have accused me of witchcraft. Not that that's much to be envied, but at least people would have believed in witches back then. Now science is the new magic and people roll their eyes if anyone admits they believe in anything that can't be explained with a formula. If you talk about the flow of energy or spirituality you get treated like a gullible airhead. It would've been nice to live in an age where you could scare people just by being able to read and have opinions."

"Up until the part where they burn you alive, of course," said the cat.

"That goes without saying."

There was a pause in which both admired a fat

bumblebee's slow flight from one flower to the next.

"Why do you have to go work?" asked Pal. "You spend almost every night dreading the next day. Then when you get home from the office you look traumatized; like you've just witnessed some terrible thing. It can't be healthy being that miserable all the time."

Eliza smiled. "I don't know what else to do, I have to pay for this house and all the tuna you eat."

The cat flopped onto the ground next to Eliza and rolled onto his side, exposing his belly, "I can't help but think you're overcomplicating things. There are other ways to pay for tuna that don't involve you being unhappy."

There was no refuting this, he was right. But the life Eliza dreamed of, she doubted existed in any job. She wanted to be a witch in a world of witches. She wanted to have a passionate romance with a handsome man and have dangerous and exciting adventures. She dreamed of sweeping around in big medieval dresses and living in an old castle that had no electricity but many roaring fires. There wasn't much chance of cackling from a broomstick flying high above the clouds by moonlight in the same world that offered suburbia and convenience stores.

"You just like to complain," continued Pal, "You could change your life if you really wanted to.

You don't change it because you're happier being miserable than you are excited about possibilities that are unknown."

Eliza said nothing as she glared out into the garden. She resented the cat. She knew Pal was right about some things, but he didn't understand how years of social conditioning were difficult to break away from. There was no use voicing this opinion out loud. He would merely accuse her of creating yet another excuse.

The cat was staring at her now. "You know there is magic, you can't keep doubting it. You're criticizing other people for not believing in it, but you've seen it with your own eyes. Why do you still think you have to live this difficult life?"

"Okay, so what if faeries and gnomes are real, and apparently sprites have been eating my raspberries?" asked Eliza. "How does that change my life in any way?"

Pal's ears folded backward with annoyance, "I've taught you how to do magic, haven't I? I can't have this conversation with you again." The cat stood and marched off into the deeper recesses of the back garden. His black tail disappeared when he slipped behind the shed.

Feeling ashamed, Eliza stared at her hand. She remembered what Pal had taught her. She closed her eyes and spread her palm on the earth beneath her. She used her soul to feel through the soil, several meters deep, until she felt moisture and free-flowing water. She scooped up the moisture using her mind and carried it back up out of the earth, feeling as it wound its way between every particle of sand, silt, and clay. She opened her eyes. It was beginning to rain in her garden. A light and totally impossible rain. Streams of water were coming upward out of the earth, swirling a couple feet above the surface, and pattering back down in a steady drizzle. Eliza smiled at the miraculous sight.

"I'm a witch," she said. The joy was short-lived. A small sadness took over her.

Not for lack of trying, Eliza found herself alone in her miracle. She had started small, reading about magical herbs and mushrooms and using crystals for energy. She read about how to use tarot cards and runes to predict the future. She had now studied every book she could get her hands on that spoke about magic, fortunetelling, and witchcraft. Eliza had tried lighting candles while in her bathtub, reciting poems above moon-charged salt with a pendulum in one hand and a broom in the other. She had an altar of magical objects where she chanted intentions. None of the wacky rituals she tried yielded any results other than a few very rare occasions. But such occasions were so rare it could be better explained by coincidence than magic.

Only when she met Pal did things begin to change.

Pal did not immediately take to Eliza, he was resentful that his previous home had given him up and he was determined not to like living with anyone else. After a while, though, Eliza let Pal out of the house to enjoy the garden with her. It was shortly after this that he began to speak to her. She learned that he had long conversations with faeries and sprites in the garden, and that they told him about a world of magic where witches and warlocks gathered at an institute to learn to use their powers. Kids were usually invited in their teens and learned to make rain, create fire, make objects disappear and use the wind to transport themselves anywhere in the world they wished to go.

"If the institute is real, why haven't they contacted *me*?" Eliza had asked when Pal told her about it. "They invite teens to study magic, why didn't I get invited?" She lamented the missed opportunity, but thought she already knew the answer to her own questions. She must not have enough magic in her for the institute to find her. It was a bitter realization, knowing she had failed even before she had begun.

The thought of a school full of happy teens manipulating the elements and flying on the breeze brought bitter tears to Eliza's eyes. It was a childhood dream that she might be whisked away during the night to Neverland, or Narnia, or transported through time with a patch of thyme! She felt anger and injustice that for other people this wasn't a dream. They actually did get to a place like Brakebills from The Magicians, or Miss Cackel's Academy for Witches like the Worst Witch. Why couldn't Eliza have this life of fantasy? Why couldn't she go to an Academy of the Unseen Arts like Sabrina?

She reached deeper into the earth and called forth *more* water to the surface. She threw the moisture as high as she could muster, feeling it gathering higher up in the sky. The sudden influx of cold water from below the earth meeting the warm September air caused friction that preceded a flash of lightning quickly followed by a rumble of thunder. Eliza stood, arms awkwardly poised either side of her as she tried to control the gathering storm. Lightning flashed three more times in such quick succession that the thunder that followed rolled into one loud clap and a long, breathless growl.

Eliza dropped her arms to her side and stumbled a bit. She placed her hand on the gooseberry bush she had planted a couple years before and borrowed some strength from it. She looked up as the dark cloud above collapsed and the rain she had created came falling down in one sudden sheet of water that immediately drenched her right through. She laughed nervously as the freezing cold water infiltrated through layers of clothes and a chill ran up her spine. The rain was over as quickly as it began. She had not really sent all that much water up, after all. Eliza wrang her long brown hair, letting the drops patter down onto the garden path.

A miserable yowl drew her attention and she burst into a fit of giggles when she saw Pal, completely soaked through. He was no longer slender and sweet, but a strange creature with eyes and ears far too big for the rest of his body. She scooped up the soaked cat and ran into the house with him cradled in her arms. They would warm up and dry themselves by the fireplace.

As Eliza's laughter disappeared from the darkening yard, she had no way of knowing that on an island some hundreds of kilometers away, an instrument made of copper and powered by magic began to whirr. A blown glass quill connected to the instrument by a long pewter rod scribbled earnestly on a sheet of paper;

ELIZA PALADIN

AGE, 28

MAGIC LEVEL 8

WINDHAM

CHAPTER TWO
The Invitation

Saturday morning dawned unseasonably damp and cold for September. Eliza wrapped herself up in her favourite housecoat and ventured out her front door. She intended only to look at her garden from the edge of the porch and watch Pal frolic among the wet plants, but an object caught her eye and kept her rooted in the doorway. A small wooden trunk, not much larger than a toolbox, had been left upon her doorstep. A card placed on top of the trunk read; *ELIZA PALADIN.*

Eliza glanced up and down the street. It was wet with oily puddles, and no one was out walking on this chilly, rainy morning. Pal darted out from the house and ran into the garden, not noticing the mysterious package. Deciding not to interrupt his fun, Eliza elected to carry the wooden box into the house and investigate the contents on her own. It was curiously light, and she carried it to her kitchen table. When Eliza removed the card with her name, it revealed the word KENTREE painted onto the trunk lid. When she opened it, she was disappointed to find the trunk was empty. It was merely a wooden box lined with velvet. But there, at the bottom, sat a fat letter.

Eliza ripped open the envelope with trembling hands. The first part of the letter was hastily scrawled by hand;

Dear Miss Paladin,

We regret to inform you that your acceptance to Kentree Institute of Magic has been overlooked for far too long. The fall semester has already begun, but with our sincerest apologies we hope you will accept a place at our school as soon as possible. With the help of faculty and classmates, we believe you will be able to catch up to your fellow students if you begin immediately.

Eliza's breath caught in her throat. It was happening. Her moment. Her call to adventure. It was really happening. The rest of the letter had the look of an impersonal mass mailing.

Kentree Institute of Magic is a place where young witches and warlocks learn to control and expand their understanding of the elements which give our people power. To be accepted, a witch or warlock must register as able to perform level 5 magic or above. If you are receiving this letter, it is because Kentree has identified you as such a person. Whether you are 15, 16, 17, or one of our rare mature students, we would be delighted to offer you a place at our school. Once *you've made your course selection after introduction week (August 31st to September 6th), you will be encouraged to purchase supplies and books from Kentree's own Quality Witching Supplies. Students are encouraged to bring whatever witching supplies they already have in order to begin the school year. A trunk has been provided with the acceptance letter as a gift.*

Students are expected to stay in school dorms during term. Courseloads are intense and practicing magic where non-magical people could witness it is strictly prohibited. If you are from a non-magical family, please find attached a blank enchanted paper. Presenting this to your parents will offer them an explanation that will satisfy any questions they may have and will make your trip to Kentree all the easier.

If you accept your invitation to study at our school, please reply by folding this letter into an airplane, and throwing it from the topmost window of your home.

Thank you,

Holly Quake

Kentree Recruiter and Assistant to the Principal

With tears forming in her eyes, Eliza re-read the letter five times over. She paused at the sentence *Whether you are 15, 16, 17, or one of our rare mature students, we would be delighted to offer you a place at our school.* She would be a mature student, then.

She read the first sentence again. *We regret to inform you that your acceptance to Kentree Institute of Magic has been overlooked for far too long.* That was curious. Was she meant to have been accepted back when she was a *'young witch'?* What did that make her now, she wondered? An old witch? An ancient hag. She laughed and shook her head. It didn't really matter. She had a miracle in her hands. She was accepted to a school of magical learning.

The sound of tapping at the window broke her from her reverie. She saw Pal mewing to be let in. Eliza crossed to the door and opened it for him. "It's chilly out there!" he exclaimed as he trotted into the warm living room. "What have you got?" he asked, spotting the letter in her hand.

"Pal, it's finally happened," laughed Eliza, bouncing on the spot. She had never felt so light and joyous in her life. Eliza read the letter aloud to Pal, stopping several times to squeal in excitement. Even Pal was thrilled, and it was difficult to get him excited about anything that didn't come from a can. He zoomed through the house, room to room, unable to contain his glee.

"You have to reply right away! They want you to start as soon as possible! We need to know where it is, how to get there—we need to pack! You have to call your parents, tell them where you're going. What are we going to do with the house?" The cat paced around the room, turning on his heel every time he thought about something else that needed to be done.

With a light-hearted chuckle, Eliza said, "Have you finally caught on that adults have responsibilities and things to do? *Of course* I want to run away to this Kentree right away, but, yeah, there's a lot to do!"

They decided, however, that everything could wait until *after* Eliza replied to the letter. She folded it into a hasty paper airplane and launched it from her bedroom window. They waited in dramatic silence for a few long seconds. The paper airplane disappeared from view almost immediately. Seconds turned to minutes, and Pal and Eliza decided they had better start packing.

"I'll need to rent out the house," said Eliza, being practical. "It wouldn't be right to leave it empty during an entire school year." She fired up her laptop and, after taking some pictures of the rooms, she published an ad on several websites renting the house until June. Once that was done, she started packing. Her runes, crystals, spirit board, and her clear crystal ball fit easily into the small wooden trunk Kentree provided (once she removed Pal who had begun taking a nap inside the box). There was a lot more room in the trunk to fill, and Eliza decided to throw in some bunches of herbs that she had been drying over the living room fire. Just in case.

Next, she packed her clothes into a suitcase and put away the rest of her personal items into boxes which she stored in the attic. Evening was closing in before anything alluding to her acceptance at a school for magic occurred. The fireplace began to make a racket. Bracing herself, Eliza wrenched open the door of the wood stove and covered her face in case anything came bursting out at her. This caution was not altogether unwarranted. A large bird made of flame, approximately the size of a goose, glided smoothly from the fire and landed upon the tiled floor. Eliza felt a pleasant warmth emanating from it. She knelt before the fiery creature and waited.

The bird opened its wings and a heavy amulet dropped from its chest and rolled on the floor until it fell to one side in front of Eliza.

"When you are ready for your journey to Kentree, hold the medallion and chant three times,

> *thoirgu eòlasmi*
>
> *thoirgu eòlasmi*
>
> *thoirgu eòlasmi*"

The fire bird folded its wings into itself and, bowing its head, its fire went out. The fire in the wood stove continued to crackle merrily behind the spot where the bird had disappeared. There was no trace left of the bird, except the hefty bronze amulet that it left behind. Pal and Eliza admired the item together, turning it this way and that so the light could catch the runes carved upon it. Eliza had the presence of mind to write down the chant on a piece of paper, lest she forget it.

It was late before Eliza went to bed. She had tirelessly packed and cleaned the house all day, while Pal watched her anxiously (it was too wet outside for exploring). Neither slept much that night. The call of adventure was too enticing. The little sleep they had was interrupted when Eliza suddenly sat bolt upright in the early hours of the morning and exclaimed that she had to quit her job.

Writing a hasty email, Eliza felt no regret or uncertainty about leaving her position. Whatever might happen, it would be better than what she was leaving behind. When she returned from her time at Kentree, however long that might be, she could find something else to do with her life. Something more meaningful. With a smile, she lay back in her bed and thought the possibilities of what she could achieve with magic were endless.

The following day, Sunday, was sunny and full of promise. After three showings of her house, a young lady in her very early twenties agreed to rent it for the school year. She was attending a university nearby and no longer wanted to share a house with four other rowdy students who did not take their studies as seriously as she did.

With one last glance at her magical garden, Eliza packed her things into her car and drove to her childhood home in Brampton to see her parents. She hugged them tightly when she arrived and presented them with the blank sheet of paper Kentree had provided her. Its effect was immediate. Their faces grew oddly blank and complacent. Eliza had only to wait.

"You're going to a hippy camp?" said her father skeptically.

"What?" asked Eliza, snatching the blank paper from him and looking at it, bewildered.

Her mother nudged him reproachfully, "Your father's just teasing. Of course, we're delighted that you're going to study to become a naturopath. It's exactly what I've been saying you should do! You have a talent when it comes to working with nature and I think you could really help people."

Eliza's eyes widened with surprise. Her mother had, in fact, been nagging her about pursuing exactly this ever since Eliza began showing an interest in gardening with herbs that healed. With a confident smile, Eliza assured her mother that she had been right and she should have listened sooner. They sat down for lunch, and chatted excitedly about the possibilities in Eliza's future. She felt giddy, like an eighteen-year-old who was going off to college for the first time. Her parents looked delighted to see her optimistic too, and this boosted her even more.

They weren't her biological parents, of course. That much was obvious just by looking at them. Her mother and father were darker in their colouring than Eliza was, and had broad strong features. Eliza occasionally envied her family for their looks. Her own wide eyes, thin mouth, and pale complexion were not likely to draw the eye. Her parents looked like athletes, while Eliza suffered from a perpetual desire to shed a few pounds. When Eliza wanted to draw attention to herself, she had to do it using her personality, rather than her physical appearance.

Being adopted was a debt Eliza could never repay. Knowing how much her parents had given her throughout her life made her feel it was all the more important to make them proud. Luckily, she was the middle child, she had an older brother and a younger sister. If she didn't make anything of herself, at least they had other children who could become successful. Seeing how happy and proud they were to discover she was returning to school to study a new career made Eliza feel strangely guilty. Her parents must have noticed how unhappy she had been in her present position and Eliza wondered if they spent their nights worrying about her, wishing they could have done more to make her a more cheerful person.

Eliza pushed away those unhelpful thoughts and concentrated on spending a lovely afternoon with her family. Finally, she gave her father her car keys and let them know she was being picked up by a friend to go to college together. With many hugs and kisses, Eliza left the house, stood out of sight behind a large shrub with her suitcase, little trunk, and Pal on her shoulder.

After having agonized the night before about how one should dress when appearing at a magical institute one month after the start of semester, Eliza had settled on what she hoped would look acceptable in any context. Sensible shoes and neckline, no flashy colours, and her hair half up in a dutch braid while loose at the bottom. She'd even gone so far as to put on a little eye-liner and blush. If there was a such a thing as a timeless look, Eliza felt she had achieved it.

She grasped the heavy amulet and retrieved the crumpled piece of paper upon which the words to the chant were written. While struggling a little with the unusual syllables, Eliza chanted,

"Thoirgu eòlasmi, thoirgu eòlasmi, thoirgu eòlasmi."

The soft breeze stopped and the air stood still for a moment. Eliza suddenly felt herself explode into a million tiny atoms. Each part of her body was spreading out at great speed across a great distance and Eliza wondered whether it would be possible ever to put herself back together again. And she became conscious that she was still having a thought, despite no longer having a brain anywhere. With a frightening whirl of great speed she felt herself appearing, thoroughly solid, in front of a great big church with huge windows of stained glass.

CHAPTER THREE
Kentree Institute of Magic

Was it one church, or several? The center one was made of red brick and boasted one large many-windowed tower. To the right was an even more impressive church made of stone with four towers. On the left was a modest church built of wood with no tower at all. The wooden church had stained glass windows, of course, but next to the brick and stone churches they looked like child's play. The ornate windows of the other two buildings were highly decorated and Eliza longed to see them from the inside where the light show would surely be greatest.

The three churches with distinct styles were patched together in a careless way. Crude passageways cut into the buildings to connect them in several places. There were tunnels from the ground level, some passages halfway up the buildings, and others connected at the roofs. The churches looked as though they had undergone some renovation; all three rooflines had been broken by the addition of many dormer windows. Two of the towers were joined clumsily by a wooden covered bridge. The original architects had created impressive places of worship, but someone without taste for beauty had really left an impression.

Overall, the impact it left upon Eliza was not a flattering one. The collection of mismatched buildings looked rundown, several windows were broken, and the roof was rotten away in some places. A fence had been erected around the front of the building which read:

"Danger—Building Unstable. Do Not Enter."

Pal twitched on Eliza's shoulder. "Not the welcome I had expected," he said with a note of disappointment.

They could hear the sound of rushing water, and Eliza was just turning to see if there was a river nearby when she heard a sound coming from the center church. A small woman with muddy brown hair came jogging down the stone steps, having appeared quite suddenly before one of the massive front doors.

"Hello! You must be Eliza," called the woman, stretching out her hand to shake Eliza's despite still being several meters away from reaching her. Eliza held out her hand uncertainly; there was still the small matter of the fence standing between the two of them. As the woman closed the gap with four long strides, Eliza gasped in surprise. The woman walked straight through the fence as though it made of air.

The woman looked quizzically at Eliza's look of astonishment while she pumped her hand in a firm handshake. "What's that look on your face?" she asked, bemused.

"You just walked through a fence," said Eliza as though it was the most obvious thing in the world.

"F—fence? Do you see a fence here?"

Now it was Eliza's turn to look suspicious, "Yeah, and great big signs that say it's dangerous to enter."

Shock and comprehension crossed the woman's face. "Oh dear," she said, "I'm afraid there is more to you than I thought!" The woman smiled pityingly at Eliza. "Here I've been racking my brain to figure out how our instruments didn't detect you for so long, and here you arrive being affected by enchantments we cast to keep Mundunces out!"

"Mundunces?"

"Just what we call people who haven't connected to their magic. Mundane dunces, originally, but eventually it was shortened to the word Mundunce," the woman replied in a professional manner. "I'm Holly, or Miss Quaker if you like, I'm assistant to the Principal and in charge of recruitment." Holly was a few years older than Eliza, approaching her forties but still in full form.

She had the firm body of someone who exercises frequently and walked with an energetic bounce in every step. Her hair was in a ponytail, and she was dressed quite like any secretary Eliza had ever seen. No swooshing cloak or pointy hat.

"When I realized you should have been accepted to Kentree over a decade ago, I was shocked! I monitor our instruments daily for signs of magical activity that could indicate a new student, and you have never registered there—"

"I'm sorry—did you just say I was supposed to be accepted over a decade ago?" interjected Eliza who felt this was a very large revelation to gloss over so quickly.

"That's right, it's very puzzling," nodded Holly. "I believe I made my apologies in your acceptance letter. A few days ago your name appears as having performed level eight magic—and at twenty-eight-years old! Highly unusual. Our instruments begin picking up low-level magic in normal circumstances. Level twos and threes start to show up and we know that we have a potential new student on our hands. But, usually, they are quite young. We do get an occasional mature student though. But it's always the same, we start seeing level two or three magic, then it grows a little bit if the person recognizes it as magic and begins working those muscles, so to speak. We send a letter of invitation in late spring to everyone who has registered level five magic. Usually kids are about fifteen or sixteen when this happens, but like I say there are always late bloomers and you will not be the oldest student here. Last year we had a woman in her seventies graduate! She was thrilled when she found out she was a witch!"

It was a lot to take in, Eliza was feeling both resentful for being overlooked for so long and grateful to finally arrive. These turbulent emotions prevented her from making further comments. Instead, she decided to absorb as much of the information as she could and would process the messy feelings later.

As Holly talked, she led Eliza into the school. Eliza walked through the security fence as Holly did and found it really was only an illusion. Walking through the front doors of the school was much the same. The doors appeared closed from outside but when Eliza crossed onto the threshold, she found the huge double doors were wide open, inviting the warm October air into the entrance chamber. From outside, the school had looked rundown and decaying. Now inside, Eliza realized the extent of the magic. There was not a single broken or boarded up window from the inside, and light poured down onto them from a large circular stained-glass window that was set high above the large double doors. Now within the hall, everything was immaculate.

"Our campus is small, and by accepting students only when they reach level five magic we are able to keep the school from overcrowding," continued Holly. "You see, if we began teaching them from the first instance of level one magic, there would be twice as many students as there are now. Most people, if they don't come from a magical family, will never develop their magic to a higher level. They could technically be trained to use magic, but as we don't have the room and their abilities haven't reached a level where they could pose a danger to themselves or society, we think it best only to teach those students who have a genuine interest in learning to use magic."

They walked through the entrance chamber and made their way down a hallway that brought them toward the back of the building. As they walked, Eliza looked through a huge doorway to her left into what had clearly been the church hall. It was now filled with round tables large enough to seat eight people at a time. Students were clustered in pairs or groups, bent over large books, scribbling into leather bound journals, or else actually performing magic. Eliza spotted a pair of boys whose faces were contorted in concentration. One had managed to conjure a ball of light in his hand but was maintaining it with some difficulty. The other boy had failed to do much of anything but continued to forcefully concentrate on the end of a large staff that he banged the end on the stone floor. Eliza's heart plummeted as she was led away from this spectacle, wanting to see more.

"You registered level eight magic the other day, which is really impressive. To achieve that level of magic without receiving training... now that could have become dangerous indeed! You've clearly been aware enough of your magic to seek out knowledge and practice on your own, but how?" Holly did not stop long enough for Eliza to answer, "I cannot imagine resources could be found in the mundane world that would teach you much about Witching. Some herbalism, possibly, it is a branch of magic that even non-magical people have been able to grasp through trial and error. Of course, a potion concocted by a witch with the same ingredients as a tea concocted by a Mundunce would have far more potent effects...

"The good news is that you are not the oldest pupil we have, despite the majority of students being in their early to late teens. A small portion of the population, perhaps three in every hundred witching folk, only begin to truly manifest their magic when they are in their twenties, thirties, sometimes not until late sixties or seventies! In those cases it is a matter of priorities. People are born with magic but want to fit in, so they suppress it and forget it is there. Then, as they age, they become restless with the mundane world they face every day. That is when they begin to cultivate their magical ability and begin to register high enough levels of magic to warrant us reaching out to them with an invitation. Some people enjoy the mundane world so much it never occurs to them to do anything else. But when their kids are grown and their careers are over and the grandchildren rarely visit... well, you will see we have several students who are here to learn about magic to complete that part of themselves they always ignored. They are not studying with the intention of ever using this magic to build a career."

Eliza did not feel it necessary to participate in the conversation Holly was having with herself, but she listened attentively to every word. She had a feeling this speech had been written for orientation week and had not been prepared only for her own benefit. Eliza exchanged a glance with Pal, who was still perched increasingly heavily on her shoulder, as Holly took in another deep breath, ready to launch back into her oration.

"I sent you an acceptance letter as soon as I saw your name on the registry. When I told the principal, well, you can understand we are both very interested. Principal Crinwere dug a little through crystal gazing and found that you had performed level three magic when you were eight years old! Why could we see that in the crystal ball, but not in the instruments? The answer is beyond me." Holly stopped in front of a stretch of blank stone wall several meters before reaching a double door that led outside through the back of the school.

"As you're already performing level eight magic, we needed to enroll you straight away. You could endanger a lot of people with that much power. Level eight and totally untrained! I can hardly believe it," Holly stopped for another deep breath. "Principal Crinwere! It's Holly with our new recruit!" Eliza looked around the empty hall, perplexed. Holly just winked animatedly at Eliza.

There was a moment when nothing happened. Then with a sound like mortar and pestle, the stones shifted to reveal a large opening in the wall that led into a comfortable and lush office apartment. The office was handsome and decorated the way Eliza imagined a secret room in a school of magic should be. Lots of thick wine-red drapery, carpets, and armchairs. There was a large stone fireplace which dominated the space and a huge clockface on one wall. The ticking was muted. An ornate wooden desk stood at one end of the room, each leg carved with the menacing face of the Green Man.

If Holly was dressed like a normal assistant, the principal made up for it by being dressed in exceeding extravagance. It was not immediately apparent to Eliza whether Principal Crinwere was a man or a woman (and she quickly wondered whether that mattered at all), and the long draping robes that billowed around them did not give much hint to the figure beneath. The principal was wearing rich shades of royal purple and blue, and wearing upon their head a delicate silver crown decorated with jewels. Whatever their gender, Eliza admired the flamboyance of the Principal's outfit.

"Welcome, Eliza," said Principal Crinwere in a deep and gentle voice, arms wide in welcome and smiling warmly at her. "I expect you have many questions. Please, be seated," Principal Crinwere indicated a comfortable armchair, and sat in a chair opposite. Eliza did as she was asked. She had a feeling this conversation was going to be longer and more intimate than usual student matriculation. Pal lay himself like a sphynx on the arm of the chair, eyeing the principal with curiosity.

The principal indicated to Holly that she was no longer needed and sent her away to take care of other school business. Eliza was treated to much the same welcome to Kentree as she had already received from Holly. Principal Crinwere recited the same speech about level five magic, and limiting the number of students in attendance. She heard again the curious circumstances of discovering they had overlooked Eliza for well over ten years.

"Yes, you should have been one of the youngest students to attend Kentree. You created level five magic when you were only twelve years old. Can you remember?"

Eliza, who had been wondering what on earth the

levels of magic could mean, thought back on what had happened when she was twelve that would have earned her a place at this school. "I pushed a group of girls down into a puddle of mud," she remembered suddenly. "They had just been teasing me that I was too ugly for Josh Hyman ever to be interested in me."

Eliza remembered the fury she felt then, watching the girls walking away from her in the school yard and feeling their whooping laughter baiting her. They were walking on the pavement, and there was a large puddle of water to one side where the lawn had been flooded with rain the day before. In her anger, Eliza wished she could dash up to them and toss them all into the muddy water. No sooner did she think it, than she felt a force of energy move through her body and shoot toward the group of girls. Like five-pin bowling, all five girls were tossed suddenly to one side and fell face first, arms outstretched, into the muddy water.

Eliza had laughed in delight that day. Even though she had been nowhere near enough to push them in, the girls had no trouble linking Eliza's maniacal laugh to the accident. The next day they held her down and beat her until she cracked two ribs. Eliza didn't go back to school for two weeks.

"How is it that this cathedral looked like a ruin until I stepped through the gate?" Eliza asked, now that the memory had reached a sour point.

Principal Crinwere considered her for a moment before answering. "It should never have appeared to you as a ruin. That is a spell we cast to keep Mundunces out. If the spell is affecting you... are you quite sure you are a witch?"

Pal saved Eliza from having to be rude, he sat up and gave the principal a look of such disgust that the principal shifted uneasily in the chair. "No, of course you are a witch. It is just unusual."

"How so?" Eliza asked. "I don't understand *why* I'm unusual. *Why* do spells aimed at mundane people work on me, and *why* didn't my magic register until last week?"

"We have been examining the instruments that detect magic ever since we discovered you to see whether there has been some tampering. Discovering a powerful witch fifteen years late is a great loss to our community. That the spell protecting the school from Mundunces affected you is yet another anomaly... Makes me wonder whether it might *not* be our instruments that have been tampered with... but you." Principal Crinwere gave Eliza a very significant look and silence hung thickly between them.

"Tell me about this cat, I can tell you share a rather special connection," said Principal Crinwere.

Eliza shrugged, "Isn't it a witch thing to have a familiar?"

"No, many witching folk have pets but to have

a familiar is a much deeper bond of connection. Does the cat help you to perform magic?"

"Help me?" Eliza laughed. "He's the one who trained me! I adopted this little runt of a cat and he hated me! But when I started to let him outside to accompany me in the garden, something changed. He began to speak to me. At first I thought I was imagining it, part of my inner monologue. Then he started saying things I was sure I wasn't imagining. There were creatures in my garden, he said. Faeries, gargoyles, gnomes. He told me about them, where to find them. I couldn't see them, but I could see the signs that they had been there. And then he taught me how to reach into myself to call on magic. You know, directing energy to do what I wanted it to. But nothing like what I saw when I walked past the Grand Room with Holly!" Eliza was dying to learn to conjure a ball of light in her bare hand.

"You cannot see faeries?" Principal Crinwere looked thoughtful for a moment but appeared to decide against continuing in that line of questioning. "You have many questions I'm sure, and many of them will be answered in your classes. I know how unfair it is for me to ask you to have patience now, considering you have been overlooked for so many years, but I am afraid it is best that you follow our usual curriculum as best as you can. You have more than likely developed some bad habits that you will need to unlearn.

You will also have much to learn about our society and how we operate within the mundane world beyond our doors.

"My new theory about how you have been overlooked is that someone has magically altered your perception and hidden you from discovery. It was, perhaps, your strong desire to be discovered as a witch that broke the charm momentarily. You could have been hoodwinked from a young age not to be able to see those signs you may have encountered in your life that prove magic is real, such as the magical creatures in your garden. Someone worked very hard to make you unfindable by witching folk and to hide your magic from yourself.

"Before anything else, you should visit the school's enchanted pool. When you swim there, all charms, spells, and curses are lifted. In order to keep you out of magical society, someone would have had to cast many spells to maintain the charade. Remove those spells now before you start your classes tomorrow. You may well have a curse placed upon you that prevents you from speaking incantations or reading our textbooks! It's best we get you free from bondage quickly. But first," Principal Crinwere slid a small pamphlet toward Eliza. "Here is the course list available for first years."

Eliza perused Kentree's course offerings for the first time while the principal busied themselves with other work.

ELEMENTAL MAGIC - Storm Soother

Learn to control the elements in this first-year course! Manipulate the power of flame to produce heat and light, and exploit the infinite power of water to create beautiful and terrible effects. No tools are required for this course apart from a sharp mind and a sharp pen!

VIBRATIONAL RESONANCE - Hystermina Cluck

Using sound and song to create magic. Everything around us is energy and has its own frequency. Learn to tune into this frequency and use it to move or break objects, grow plants, and heal broken hearts. Ability to carry a tune required, perfect pitch strongly recommended if students desire to move on to second year.

HERBALISM - Willow Walker

Growing, caring, harvesting, and storing herbs magical and mundane for use in potions, spells, and protection. Learn during which phases of the moon plants are most potent to harvest, and how to water them to maximize yield! In this starter course you will get cut, pricked, tangled, and occasionally poisoned by a plant masquerading as an innocent herb! Course requirements: mortar and pestle, good secateurs, string, a drying rack or shelf, and mason jars.

COOPERATION WITH BEINGS MAGICAL AND MUNDANE - Hazel Brown

This first-year course covers the basics of communication with creatures magical and mundane. By the end of the first year, you will understand the psychology of most animals which are commonly met. Ever wanted to spy on a neighbour? Or else destroy their prize lettuce without leaving any trace? You will be able to become fast friends with wolves, use birds to convey messages, and tell rabbits where they ought to have a good meal (and more importantly to please leave your cabbages well alone). Students who continue in this field of study through until fourth year will be among the few who will learn to transform themselves into animals. Course requirements: a wand, staff, or other magical amplification device.

SORCERY - Mark Kent

Why complicate life when there is an incantation for that? Wand magic is all you need, just twirl the wand, say a few words and Presto! Anything is possible, even if your magic is as weak as a watered-down cup of tea. Easier to learn and master than most other branches of magic. We will cover practical, combative, healing, and destructive spells in this course. There are no limits to what you can do when you have a wand! Course requirements: a wand, notebook, and pen.

HEALING – Nepi Teget

Learn to detect sources of pain and how to heal them. This course combines practices which can be learned in Herbalism, Sorcery, Vibrational Resonance, and Potions but does so with a focus on healing. Students interested in specializing in Healing in their fourth year are encouraged to enroll in the aforementioned courses to gain a fuller understanding of these branches of magic and the ingredients involved. It is the noblest of professions. Requirements: strong academic mind capable of reading several hours per day and memorization. Verify course requirements for Herbalism, Sorcery, Vibrational Resonance, and Potions for a complete list.

TRANSPOSITION – Siobhan Neach

In the first year you will learn to move objects with your mind. Shock and dazzle Mundunces by making a table float across the room (you must pretend it is only an illusion, of course). By the end of the first year, you will move on to teleporting objects small distances of up to a few hundred meters. Students who continue into the third year will learn to teleport themselves distances up to several hundred kilometers. Requirements: none, but some students perform better with a wand, staff, or other magical amplification object.

FORTUNE TELLING – Hystermina Cluck

Predict the future, become a soothsayer, speak in prophecy and riddles! Fortune telling is one of the most gratifying branches of magic. People are drawn to soothsayers as much as they are terrified of us. In this course we will use runes, tarot, tea leaves, crystal pendulums and spirit boards to unravel the mysteries of the future. Students who move on to study the course in following years will learn palm reading, crystal gazing, astrology, and eventually progress to telling the future merely by touching an object that belongs to the querent. Course requirements: first year students require a set of runes, tarot cards, a spirit board, and crystal pendulum. Tea will be provided for you.

ENERGY AMPLIFICATION – Rodney Stone

Learn about the qualities of wood, crystals, and metals and how to use these to craft your own wands, staffs, spirit boards, pendulums, medallions, and crowns. It is common knowledge that witching folk can better direct and augment their magical energy with the use of these tools. This is the course for those who like to work with their hands. Course requirements: there is a fee for this course which will be waived if you produce three instruments of high enough quality that can be made available for sale in Kentree's Quality Witching Supplies by the end of your first year.

EMPATHOLOGY AND MENTALISM – Derren Angel

In this course you will learn to read a mind, communicate voicelessly with a peer, see someone's memories, receive and interpret people's emotions. As you progress to other years, you will learn to influence the emotions in a room and even control and possess a human mind.

POTIONS – Willow Walker, Nepi Teget, and Principal Rowan Crinwere

Potions are as versatile as wand magic but with the

advantage that they can be bottled and preserved for later use. They can be shared with witching folk less adept than yourself, and can save you or restore you when your own magic is spent. This course is jointly taught by three professors. Course requirements: enrolment in Herbalism. A cauldron. A set of potions ingredients, glass bottles, sealing wax, and a wooden paddle.

NECROMANCY – Arius Claeg

Speak with those who have gone beyond our world. Bring the temporary apparition of people who have passed. Release ghosts from purgatory. Trap free spirits into this world as a curse and animate corpses. This magic is for those of sharp mind and steady moral compass. Much of the magic covered in the three years of Necromancy is prohibited in the wider magical world. This is the only Necromancy course offered anywhere in the world. It is recommended study for those wishing to become a Wizard. This course also has a high expulsion rate. We do not tolerate morally dubious characters in this class. Requirements: a set of crystals, a crystal ball, a wand, and full set of candles.

Eliza devoured the list and when she was finished she looked up at the principal ready to burst with a million questions. Principal Crinwere raised a hand to silence her.

"Fourth year is when you can get into really specialized courses and the magic becomes not just a brute force but an elegant thing of beauty. Students begin with a full courseload of six classes their first and second year, and then focus on three branches of magic by their third year. Their final year they either only study one branch or else choose to graduate after year three and forego the final year altogether. Your first two years are generally free to try any of the courses that interest you so that you can make that choice in the third year. The allure of wand work which you will learn in Sorcery may seduce you at first, but when you realize harnessing the power of flame in Elemental Magic can produce many of the same results you will feel more comfortable walking away from one subject toward another."

"—sorry to interrupt. Some of the courses here only have three years, and others have four years? At least, that's what it looks like in the pamphlet."

"Correct. Even if you only enroll in Necromancy your second year, you could still choose that subject as your specialty for fourth year."

"What does it mean by *It is recommended study for those wishing to become a Wizard*?"

Principal Crinwere explained that Wizards are those peculiar folk who have mastered all forms of known magic. There are fewer than two dozen true Wizards in the world. These obsessives spend their lives discovering new branches of magic and perfecting them. Wizards are the magical authority who keep witching folk (a blanket term for all people with harnessed magical ability) in check with the laws of the world. To become a Wizard, one acquires much natural wisdom and so Wizards are seldom tempted by evil. They are merely the balance that brings the world to order.

"Some students enjoy learning so much that they choose not to graduate until they have taken, or attempted, all the courses we offer. They might go on to another magical institute which offers different courses and continue their education there. This is a very exciting place for those of academic mind." Principal Crinwere smiled at Eliza who was reaching forward to take the pamphlets with course descriptions for years two, three, and four. She was drinking it all in with her mouth open in shock. It was everything she had ever dreamed of.

"I want to learn all of it!" she exclaimed.

Principal Crinwere laughed gently. "Why don't I have Holly take you to the enchanted pool and have those barriers removed from your mind? We shall meet again in the morning to finalize your timetable and get anything you require from our supply shop. It would be a good idea if you could meet some students this evening and ask them which courses they are taking, and see what interests you most."

CHAPTER FOUR
The Enchanted Pool

Eliza found herself on a path behind the old cathedrals, Holly having led her there. She was told to go straight until she reached the enchanted pool. "It should only be a thirty-minute walk," Holly had smiled at her before bouncing back toward the school buildings. Eliza's faithful cat lead the way with tail upright in curiosity. The gardens just outside the school were neatly clipped and perfectly symmetrical. The straight path guided toward a kissing gate, on the other side of which the gardens became less formal.

Like an English cottage garden, explosions of colour overflowed from their borders. The many plants whose flowers had faded had been clipped back leaving the ones still in bloom in centerstage. It had the look of a carelessly planned garden, as if the gardener had planted as many species combinations as possible there without much thought to a unified theme. The effect made the garden look effortlessly beautiful, so much so that

Eliza was certain a lot of effort had been taken to achieve the feat.

Following her cat down the path through the garden, the flower beds gave way to an orchard garden. Apple trees and pear trees in espaliers enclosing rows and rows of berry bushes on either side of the path. It was a few minutes more before they found themselves surrounded by a forest, trees creaking merrily in the fall breeze. Autumn was in full force here, leaves glowed in shades of yellow, red, and orange. The sound of running water was also present in the woods, though Eliza never lay eyes on the river.

Still they walked on, past innumerable mushrooms which sprouted through fallen leaves in the undergrowth. The forest changed from oak and maple to dense evergreens, then thick brush. The path became narrow and Eliza's clothes began to catch on menacing thorns growing from the tips of sinister branches. Now hot from the walk, clammy and having ignored several tempting forks in the path, Eliza was grateful to emerge from a bend to this route's conclusion. Burrs were sticking to her clothes as she stripped off her scarf and jacket, face flushed.

The clearing looked like a dream. The path disappeared to reveal a meadow of wild grasses in the middle of which was a wide pool of water. There were three large weeping willows around the edge of the pond, their long limbs draping lazily on the surface of the water, leaves still green in the fading light.

Eliza did not hesitate. Not only was daylight fading fast but she felt compelled to seek her truth. Learning that someone had cast spells upon her to impede her introduction to the magical world felt an intrusion. She felt dirty. Tainted. Itchy. What possible motive could someone have had to prevent her from living a life of magic and splendor? She had known she was able to do something special, but in a world of monotony and doing as you're told, she had never been permitted to reach her full potential.

Eliza felt vindicated in discovering she was not alone in feeling the forces of nature in the very fiber of her being. She could not wait to learn to control them. When these enchantments were washed away—curses, she thought to herself—her next priority (aside from vigorously taking on the challenging studies ahead of her) would be to discover exactly who it was who had been pulling the strings of her life since she was a small child. She would lift the veil from her eyes, then find the person who put it there.

Eliza's clothes landed softly in the overlong grass as she approached the water. She had agonized over how she would dress for her first day as an official 'witch'. It seemed so stupid now. None of that superficial stuff mattered. The only thing that mattered was accepting and becoming her true self. Her foot slid into the water's edge.

To say it was cold would be an understatement. "Oh bloody fudge!" she cried. The cold stung her skin. From habit, she began to draw energy from the earth, the air, and the water to warm herself but Pal interrupted her concentration.

"I wouldn't bother trying a spell to protect yourself from the cold," he said. "This water is made to wash away enchantments. Don't fight it. Calm your mind and accept the cold."

Eliza grudgingly admitted the cat was right. She let the spell she had started to weave fall away; the energies she had called upon dissipated. She took a deep, steadying breath and tried to accept the cold as she walked further into the pool. The icy water was biting at her ankles and legs. She could no longer feel her feet. She waded into the middle of the pool, the water barely reaching the top of her thighs.

"You have to submerge yourself," called the cat from the water's edge.

Eliza would have rolled her eyes except she was trying to stop her teeth from chattering. It had been perfectly obvious that she would have to submerge herself, but it didn't make the task any easier. Her lips were turning blue from the cold. The air had felt lovely and warm when they were walking. She could not believe only moments ago she was overwarmed. "You try it," Eliza hissed at the cat.

Even so, though it was the last thing she wanted to do, Eliza forced herself onto her knees. The water lapped up her thigh and kissed her belly. She yelped from the shock and decided not to prolong the inevitable. She plunged face forward into the icy cold water and let it submerge her completely.

Once under the water, it didn't seem so bad. There were lights here. Houses. Tiny creatures swarmed around her brandishing pitchforks. These ones had tails and wild hair. Others had legs and looked nearly human. The humanish creatures rode on the backs of giant koi fish using their whiskers as reins. Eliza giggled. It was a silly sight.

There was something else, too, in the distance. Something that looked like a castle with a great stone tower. Eliza reached forward and upon doing so she realized she was not a huge human in a small pool, but she had become as small as the water sprites that swam around her.

The castle in the water looked miles away now. She had a nagging feeling that within this castle lay the answers she was looking for. The mystery person who had cast her out of the magical world and hid her from it was in the tower standing by the light. Eliza was just too far to make them out. She reached forward and began swimming toward the light. Her body glided forward effortlessly in the water. She hadn't felt the need to breathe since she submerged herself.

Deeper and deeper she went, swimming through dark waters. She reached the castle after only a minute and swam over its many courtyards. Eliza was just nearing the tower when dark spots appeared in her vision. She blinked stupidly, trying to fix her eyes upon the person in the tower but her lungs started to pain her. Eliza clutched her chest as realization overtook her. She was running out of oxygen.

She opened her mouth and it filled with water, unpleasantly cold. She glanced up at the sky, the last moments of sunset glittering through the rippling surface looked miles away. She tried to swim toward the surface but her arms were heavy and tired. She couldn't control her frozen legs. She looked down at them helplessly and tried to kick but they remained painfully still. Beginning to panic, Eliza realized with a start that the water sprites had led her to her death. Never able to see them until today and now a victim of their malicious tricks.

A sharp bite on her ear made her push backward with her arms and legs reactively. Her intake breath of surprise caught her when she was still under the water so as her head broke the surface she began choking on a lungful of water. She retched and coughed until the water left her lungs and she turned her attention to the pain she was now feeling on her back and shoulder. Pal was clinging to her, his claws leaving watered down blood trickling down her chest and back as he struggled to stay on. He was soaking wet, again.

"You—what—what happened?" Eliza spluttered to the spiky animal on her shoulder.

"You were an idiot—that's what. Get out of this stupid swamp and we can talk about it," the cat growled back at her. Eliza transferred Pal from her shoulder with some difficulty. He was all claws and the scratches were particularly painful on her bare skin. She managed to get him to cradle in her arms but even so, his claws were out as ever and she soon had scratches on her forearms and chest too.

Eliza's joints protested as she made her way back to the bank. Once out of the water, the cat swatted at her frozen skin and demanded "Dry us. Quick." His wet fur gave him a mad, bug-eyed look. Eliza obeyed Pal's order as quickly as she could.

She struggled to make her frozen fingers work. She spread them out, her whole body trembling uncontrollably, and began feeling into the water on her skin and on Pal wishing the energy to redirect itself into the air and into the ground beneath them. She felt the water trailing off them both with unnatural quickness. Her hair dried and the black cat began to loosen its grip. She continued until she felt the sticky wet fur become light and fluffy on her cheek. Pal leapt onto the ground. Eliza's shoulder stung from the scratch wounds.

Eliza looked at the black cat. "What happened in the pool? I thought I was miles deep when you bit me."

Pal made a most patronizing face and fixed her with a steady gaze. "You were drowning face down in a pond three feet deep. All you had to do was sit up. I should be asking *you* what happened." The cat made an angry sort of growl. "I waited awhile, hoping you'd come back out, but you kept thrashing around and then... you seemed to be losing the fight."

"Oh Pal," said Eliza, slipping her clothes back on. "I've never seen a sprite before—or any sort of magical creature. Can you believe the first ones I see with my own eyes almost killed me? I was sure there was something important at the bottom of the pool... I was being lured to my death."

Pal gave himself a vigorous shake to make all his hair settle down correctly, and gave Eliza another condescending look, "You followed a light, didn't you? *Never* follow strange lights!"

Eliza finished dressing and looked at her cat with sadness. "I'm sorry I made you come in after me."

"It's fine," said the cat, "just as long as I still get some tuna every night and you keep humouring me when I attack your ankles from behind the curtains I'll be happy."

With a small smile, Eliza scooped Pal into her arms and hurried back up the path toward the school. The forest was quickly plunging into darkness. On the walk back they saw faeries, gnomes, and faces in the trees which whispered into the evening air. After her unpleasant encounter with the water sprites Eliza was not much interested in engaging with these creatures. She broke into a jog, and dropped Pal gently to the forest floor to trot along ahead of her. It was with relief she returned to the school to find Holly, who would take her to her dorm.

CHAPTER FIVE
Herbalism

Of the three old churches, the stone one with four towers had been converted entirely into student residences. Eliza's dorm room was on the second floor, and she was lucky to have one quarter of a stained-glass window spilling light into her room.

Holly told Eliza the students on the third story were the luckiest. They had dormer windows with clear glass and views out onto the river that surrounded the school. Being on the second story, the large stained-glass windows had been divided in half for the upper and lower floors, then divided again so that the room next to Eliza shared the other quarter of the same window. The part of the window that appeared in Eliza's room showed the image of a lamb and a bowl of grapes. The words "The Lord shall Be—" were written there but cut off by the wall. She would have to make friends with the neighbour to find out how that sentence ended.

They didn't stay long in her room, just long enough for Holly to place Eliza's suitcase and trunk on a wooden desk and for Eliza to take in her new digs. It was only slightly larger than typical college dorms rooms, but furnished in much the same way. One desk, one chair, two wall-mounted shelves. A single bed. There was a closet, and a rug on the wood plank floor. The lights flickered when turned on, but after a few moments settled into a steady illumination with a faint hum. Eliza would share a bathroom with other students, it was just down the hall from her room.

Holly rushed Eliza back down a flight of stairs to a small shop on the ground floor called Kentree Quality Witching Supplies.

"Some students order things by mail from other shops. Things here are a touch more expensive than you'll find elsewhere. But that's the price of convenience. I just wanted to show you the shop because you'll likely need to buy some things for your classes tomorrow. But it's also here that you'll get your first free staff or wand. Do you have a preference?"

"Does it make a big difference which I choose?"

"A wand is easier to carry around, but otherwise no, there is no difference. A staff also makes a good walking stick," answered Holly.

Eliza decided, "I think I'd prefer a wand."

Holly smiled and rushed Eliza through to the back of the shop into what looked like a supply closet. The shopkeeper did not even bother to look up from the book he was reading to see what they were up to. What Eliza took to be a supply closet was a small room filled with crowns, staffs, wands, amulets, and talismans. There was so much to look at Eliza had no idea where to begin.

"Kentree makes some of its money selling the herbs, potions, and amplification tools that students make at the school. That's how we can offer a free education. Of course, educating witching folk is also good for business! When you graduate and want a potion that you remember took you four months to brew, you might decide it's a better use of your time just to order a bottle instead of brewing it yourself."

As a new student, Eliza was allowed to choose one wand to begin her classes. If she decided to take Energy Amplification, the tool making class, she might soon replace her wand with one of her own making. Or else, she could purchase a new wand whenever she liked. When Eliza asked about the crowns, Holly tutted impatiently. "Those are great for when you've covered the basics and want to really amp up your game. As a first year you'll barely have control on what you're doing—the last thing we want is to amplify energy you can't control yet! You can look at those in your third year."

There were many wands to choose from. All different types of wood, some burnt with runes and symbols or phrases, others had crystals embedded in the handle or on the tip. One jet black wand had a fissure filled with gold. Eliza was quite drawn to that one, but in the end chose a simple wand. It looked to be made of Yew, it was as long as her forearm and fit comfortably into her hand.

Holly dragged Eliza out of the closet and showed her a belt rack. There were leather belts with wand holsters, "Since you chose a wand, you'll need one of these. But you can buy that with the rest of your things tomorrow morning. Do you remember the way to your room?" Eliza nodded. "Great, I've got to dash, lots to do in the evening. I expect I'll be seeing you tomorrow when you choose your courses. Welcome to Kentree!"

Eliza loved the feeling of the wand in her hand, and stood for a few minutes in the shop admiring the sensation. It wasn't until the shopkeeper barked at her that he wanted to close if she wasn't going to buy anything that Eliza left the store. She walked back to her room, admiring her wand all the way. Even Pal wanted to rub his cheeks against it. Of course, Eliza had no idea what to do with the stick and when she waved it nothing happened.

After washing up and putting on some fresh clothes, Eliza walked back through the school toward the Grand Room she had seen on her way in. Holly told her that was where meals were taken. There were only a few other students in the halls as Eliza made her way. They looked impossibly young to be teenagers, and Eliza felt self-conscious about her age. The other students were dressed not unlike anyone in the outside world, Eliza noted. There were no fabulous medieval gowns among the teens, but there was a certain modesty in the clothes that gave the impression of older fashions.

Kentree looked even grander now after her time in the enchanted pool. Eliza suspected this was a different sort of enchantment. Like magic was holding the old building together rather than true craftsmanship. She made a detour on her way to supper to return to the spot where she knew Principal Crinwere's office was hidden. Reaching the stone wall, Eliza felt the area with her hand. Her fingers met a pleasant tingling warmth where they touched the stone. She smiled. In a world where magic and illusion are part of daily life, she wondered how much of what you could see and feel could be trusted.

Once in the Grand Room, Eliza kept an eye out for displays of magic but most students were more intent on eating than performing. This room was a large open hall where students and staff mingled together. Holly had told her this served as mess hall and study hall between meals. The alcove, which used to be the church altar upon which a pastor would have read the daily mass, was now a small library whose bookshelves went all the way up the height of the ceiling, some thirty feet high. There were a few ladders available for students to peruse the higher shelves if they had not yet mastered the art of self-levitation.

Eliza's gaze moved above the tables to find the source of the hall's illumination. There were no electric bulbs in this room, what lit the tables below were glowing orbs of light floating high above the heads of the diners.

After wandering around the edge of the room for a minute, Eliza realized she would have to make the uncomfortable decision of where to sit. She started paying more attention to the students now and tried to imagine to which group she might belong. There was a table of witches that all looked about seventeen with long shimmering blonde hair and chatting as animatedly as birds. A table of young warlocks, insulting one another loudly in a show of masculine bravado befitting newly pubescent boys. She spotted a table of crones, no that wasn't fair, these must be the mature students of which Holly had spoken. Ladies in their sixties and seventies who were learning magic for the first time. Eliza smiled at the thought of joining their table. She would keep them as a backup plan.

Finally, Eliza chose her target. She walked past a table where a skinny, translucent witch sat with what appeared to be a yeti, to arrive at a table of students that looked a little more varied. Three girls and three boys in their early twenties who might therefore be more mature than the teenagers Eliza passed over.

"Hiya, mind if I sit here?" asked Eliza shyly. The students gave her an appraising look and allowed her to join them. Most of them continued their conversation, ignoring Eliza totally as she helped herself to some stew. Luckily one of the girls was curious about why Eliza was joining the school a month late and was very glad to offer Eliza her thoughts on which classes she should take.

Patty, a plump witch with an upturned nose, had very strong opinions about the courses at Kentree that Eliza should avoid. The basis of most of her arguments for or against any class was how easy or difficult the magic was to control. She was in her second year already and went so far as to tell Eliza which were the "easy" teachers, and which were not.

"The thing is, a lot of the classes overlap," explained Patty, helping herself to a generous portion of dessert. "See, Herbalism isn't so different from Potions once you have the ingredients in hand. And Sorcery, where you do magic with a wand and an incantation, completely removes the need for Elemental Magic. Some people like the grand feeling of being taken over by power and unleashing it, but why bother? You could just point a wand at the problem and say a word. No need for meditative power or mindfulness like *Vibrational Resonance*." Patty's emphasis on the words made it clear she did not think much of the subject. She spooned more pudding into her mouth and said, "Even Potions, really. Most of the potions you learn to brew could be replaced with a spell and a wave of a wand."

It was late when Eliza had read the course descriptions ten times over and made her final choices. Six courses were the maximum a student could take in their first year and Eliza was determined not to miss an opportunity to learn. There were some classes she wouldn't be able to take this year as they overlapped with others on the timetable, but she could take them the following year. In the end she chose the following six courses:

ELEMENTAL MAGIC

HERBALISM

COOPERATION WITH BEINGS MAGICAL AND MUNDANE

SORCERY

TRANSPOSITION

ENERGY AMPLIFICATION

She smiled, satisfied. It was late when she turned off the lights and tried to sleep. It was another night interrupted by many dreams. Eliza woke several times in a panic, fearing she had slept through her first class. Poor quality sleep notwithstanding, Eliza woke up early the following morning feeling totally energized. Never in her life had she been more excited about anything than she was about starting her new courses.

"These are excellent choices for your first-year," Principal Crinwere told her, "Good basics and a lot of room for exploration into different specialties as the years progress. Some students choose to focus in their very first year and it is difficult for them when they realize they weren't all that talented in their chosen field!"

"Does that often happen?" Eliza asked.

"Oh yes, you will likely notice within the first month that some magic seems intuitively to suit you. You will find some subjects easy and natural. Just as other subjects will feel like a chore and impossibly difficult. Often we gravitate towards those subjects for which we have a natural talent."

Eliza nodded in agreement, remembering how Patty described her own course preferences, but she was secretly terrified of not excelling in all her classes. It had never crossed her mind that she might not be *good* at magic. She was determined to excel, natural talent be damned.

Her first class was Herbalism. She felt optimistic about this course, certain she was already advanced in the subject. She was sure she would have a chance to impress the professor from the get-go and earn the respect of her fellow students.

Unfortunately, destiny had other plans.

Eliza's first class made it clear she knew nothing of magical plants. There were scores of sentient plants and plants that could only grow if the seed was fed a potion beneath a blood moon while someone murmured an ancient chant. Her knowledge of mundane plants and their properties was vast, but there were many more plant species in the magical world that she had never heard about.

In her first lesson, they were told they would be harvesting leaves from conscious plants called Hochelaga. These plants could move and did not particularly enjoy having their leaves plucked.

"Ouch!" gasped Eliza as a vine from a Hochelaga plant whipped her hand derisively. She had been trying to remove two lemon-scented, gold hued leaves from one of its limbs. A fellow student had just plucked leaves from a neighbouring Hochelaga in the school's gardens and the plants were quickly sounding the alarm to one another. The vines which were so calm when the students arrived were now whipping about violently.

Eliza tried reaching into the magic of the plant, closing her eyes and focusing her energy toward the life force in the Hochelaga. When she reached its conscious thought-center she had a blurry vision of a terrified and defensive soul. She tried to send it loving and caring thoughts in the hopes of calming it long enough to get a few leaves, but the plant's mind responded in attack.

Eliza tripped over her feet and fell onto her backside in the damp grass after the shock of mental attack. Determined, she tried to reach the plant again using soothing energies. The life force of the Hochelaga trembled and paused to listen as she tried to explain wordlessly the intention was only to take a couple of leaves and not to take the plant's life. She received in response an agonized "Whyyyyy?" and the soul of the plant clearly communicated the pain of losing even just two leaves to her. The emotion she received from the plant was so overwhelming that Eliza dissolved into panicked tears.

"Stop!" she called out to the other students. "You're hurting them!"

But to Eliza's surprise, she was not the only one who had a change of heart. Several other students appeared to have attempted communicating with the plants and were attacking the ones who had not tried this approach. Or else they were huddled in the fetal position and crying in agony while clutching their heads.

Professor Walker, a hardened little old woman whose skin was so weathered she appeared to have been carved out of wood, chuckled to one side of the group of panicking students. Eliza noticed this and stumbled toward her. "What is the lesson here?" Eliza demanded. "Are we supposed to harvest leaves from a plant knowing the pain it causes them?"

A few other students stopped to listen to the exchange. Professor Walker stepped forward into the thicket of Hochelaga plants. She dodged a few whipping vines and danced among the plants, evading their thrashing limbs. Light on her toes, Professor Walker weaved through the rows of lemon-y golden leaves and ducked beneath them when they came too close to striking her. She finally emerged in front of the class with only a small cut beneath her eye. She wiped away a thick drop of blood from the fine cut and produced from the pockets of her dress a few dozen large golden leaves.

"Go ahead and speak to the plants, see whether they felt their leaves parting from them," commanded the little professor.

The students all closed their eyes in unison and attempted communication with the angry plants again. When they opened their eyes, they confirmed that no, not one of the vines had noticed a leaf being taken from them apart from the one that first sounded the alarm.

"Plants require pruning, dividing, mowing, and harvesting to grow into their full potential. It may seem cruel to uproot a sapling that is growing too close to a mature tree, but this discomfort is essential so that it may thrive when transplanted to a new area with less competition. Just as a mother suffers nine months of pregnancy and hours of painful childbirth in order to continue her family, so does the plant have to suffer to live a long and prosperous life with many descendants.

"Some plants will perish immediately when they go to seed. By regularly pruning the plant we prevent it from producing ripe seeds. Are we being cruel? The plant would only have lived a few months. Thanks to our intervention it has now been blessed with a life many years longer than its natural instincts would have allowed.

"Hochelaga plants are conscious, and when they communicate to each other that they are under attack, they all go into a panic. They feel the vibration of your heavy footsteps on the earth and they fear what you will do to them. Fear drives them into a frenzy. They distrust the manipulation you attempt when you reach to them with magic. They respond aggressively." Professor Walker made her way through the students and picked up a small stone from the ground.

"If I hit you with a rock without warning you might feel pain, depending on the size of the rock. But if I threaten you with the rock—" Professor Walker held the stone behind her shoulder and prepared her body as if she was gearing to throw the stone in full force at a pupil, who recoiled in anticipation, "—what would you do? You would flinch, as Chad here has just demonstrated." A few girls giggled until Professor Walker feigned launching the stone in their direction and they screamed. "You might cry out in anticipation of potential pain—or you might beg me not to throw the rock at all. The fear of potential harm causes greater anxiety than the actual action. These plants did not notice me harvesting their leaves because they were so busy throwing a tantrum they couldn't sense me among them." Professor Walker let the stone drop back to the ground and clapped her hands together.

"Now, take these leaves—two each. We will be learning about their properties and how to use them for a few potions and spells. Follow me back to the classroom."

By the time Eliza went for lunch in the early afternoon, her head ached. It had been years since she had set foot in a classroom and a four-hour lesson was a long time to try to absorb new information. Luckily, she didn't have another class until the following afternoon so she would have time to read the pile of material Professor Walker had given her. Eliza needed to catch up on a month of schoolwork she had missed.

Head pounding from trying to stuff it full of new information, unfamiliar vocabulary, and impossible magic became the norm for Eliza over the next few weeks. She was a month behind in every subject and totally out of practice as a student. Leaves celebrated October by creating a riotous display of colour which drew students to spend these precious fall days out of doors. Eliza envied them as she spent her hours rubbing her neck from the strain of bending it over so many books. She had never considered herself old before, but being surrounded by young teens who absorbed information like sponges made her feel positively ancient.

After her first supper had been shared with Patty they did not eat together again. Patty was frequently locked into a passionate embrace with her boyfriend Beau, and Eliza had the sense she was not welcome at most tables. Even the older women whom she had judged as friendly crones made the spare chair from their table disappear suddenly when Eliza began to approach them on her second day at the school.

Over the first few weeks, Eliza tried sitting with a few different groups of students at mealtimes, but nothing clicked. When students allowed her to join them at their table, she was sure that they were merely tolerating her presence. No one engaged her in conversation. It wasn't until her third week she decided to join the transparent witch and the yeti. Faye Griggs and Mashu Menengai, respectively.

Eliza had quite given up on making any new

friendships by this point. Besides, she was completely absorbed in her coursework and her desire to prove herself. She had no time for idle conversation and laughter, as the other students did. She felt harried by her ever-growing pile of homework so when she sat to join Faye and Mashu for supper one day, it was without intention of joining their conversation.

Mashu was a peculiar looking creature. He was less than five feet tall, had broad shoulders nearly as wide as he was tall and long arms that reached his knees. His face was nearly obscured by thick white fur that appeared to cover his entire body. He moved awkwardly and without grace, such that Eliza suspected wearing clothing and shoes were not in his usual nature.

The other student, Faye, was equally strange but dazzling in her beauty. She was hard to focus on, she shimmered as if lighter than air. A petite witch with pearly skin that glowed like the moon, her eyes narrow and dark. Eliza suspected Faye to have a large pair of wings like an overgrown butterfly but try as she might, she could never focus her eyes upon them. She was certain the wings were there in her peripheral vision.

The pair did not speak to Eliza that first day, but it was a comfortable silence in which they all remained seated at the table together long after supper had ended. They studied until half past eleven, and when Mashu rose to leave, he wished both Faye and Eliza a good evening. The girls made eye contact then, and Faye rose shortly after Mashu and bade Eliza a goodnight, too. From then on, Eliza counted herself among a table of friends.

CHAPTER SIX

Mark Kent

Eliza spent more hours with her nose in a book, writing essays, practicing wand movements, and memorizing chants and incantations than any other Kentree student that October. She became obsessed with acquiring knowledge and becoming equal to her younger classmates—with increasing frustration. Weeks passed and she only kept falling further behind. She was frustrated with the Sorcery course, which according to most students was the easiest form of magic. For Eliza, however, this course proved to be the most difficult.

Her third week at Kentree she held up a hand during a Sorcery class.

The professor, a handsome young wizard who had an English accent and floppy hair, paused in his lecture. He was wearing a three-piece brown suit which tried to hide the slight paunch he had around the middle, with little success.

"—yes?"

"I'm sorry to interrupt," said Eliza, bursting with annoyed impatience as Professor Kent had just revealed a fresh list of spells they were expected to master by the following week. "It's just—maybe you already covered this when you began the course, but—I wondered what is the advantage to casting spells, hexes, charms and curses with a wand as opposed to using the raw forces of nature to create magic? It's just—I mean, I might be wrong but—it seems to me raw magic is more powerful than the magic that can be cast with a wand."

Professor Kent smiled. "Miss Paladin, I'm delighted you've removed your face from that book long enough to ask a question." Eliza snapped shut the huge journal she had been using to keep track of all the spells and wand movements they were being assigned every week. "There is truly no better way to learn than to challenge the status quo!" he said. "Please stand up at the back of the classroom and face me."

Eliza did so apprehensively. She had a feeling Professor Kent was toying with her like a cat plays with a mouse. She braced herself for public humiliation.

Professor Kent placed a stool in the middle of the classroom and with a wave of his wand conjured a crystal champagne flute. He stepped back to the front of the class and addressed Eliza, "I expect that by now you know how to create water using the elements?"

"Yes, I've been able to make it rain since before I came to Kentree." The smallest hint of a brag entered her voice.

"Do you know how to create water with a wand and incantation?"

"Uh—not yet, I don't think we've covered that yet."

"I shall tell you the incantation, and you will fill the glass *using the incantation*. This is the wand movement you shall use." He demonstrated by swooping his wand downward and dragging it gently back toward his chest *"Aquari,"* he said with a clear and deliberate voice. The glass filled gently with water until it was full.

"Aquari," repeated Eliza. "Okay, I think I can do that."

Professor Kent emptied the glass with a sharp twitch of his wand, and indicated with an inviting gesture that he was ready whenever she was. Eliza gripped the yew wand she had been provided and readied herself.

"Aquari" said Eliza with confidence, and she copied the wand movements she had watched the professor perform. The glass filled with water but did not stop. Water spilled over the top of the champagne flute and onto the stool before Eliza could control the spell and stop the water filing the glass and spilling onto the floor.

"Very good, fairly easy you might say. Though you had never performed the spell before, by having the step-by-step instructions you were able to perform it quite well. I'm sure with only a few more tries you could perfect it," said Professor Kent encouragingly, strolling around the room as he spoke.

His eyes swept around his younger pupils. "Not to worry, some of you will need more than one try to get any water but this is due to your age and power limitations. As Eliza is a mature student, we can expect that she will have a firmer grasp of the magic she carries." There was something in his tone when he said 'mature student' that Eliza couldn't quite put her finger on.

Professor Kent emptied the glass again and was back at the front of the class. He gave Eliza a smile that bordered on flirtatious which gave her a pleasant whooping sensation in her stomach. "Please try to fill the glass using elemental magic," he told her.

Eliza smiled to herself. This was going to be easy; she had been producing water for her garden for months. She felt the atmosphere around the room and below her feet, down into the earth and invited moisture to come toward her. The energy filled her chest and she opened her eyes and looked at the delicate champagne flute on the stool. With a jolt, she realized there was no way she could fill it without causing it to rain in the entire classroom.

She tried to redirect the energy within her as gently as she could toward the glass in a thin stream, but even so she could not control the power enough to get near the glass without knocking it over. Her face contorted with concentration and wind kicked her hair around. The students near her had to dive after their books as the force of the wind picked up and tossed their belongings onto the floor.

Eliza was not ready to give up on a challenge. She continued trying to control the flow of water and create a smooth path from herself to the glass. She cupped both her hands in front of her in an attempt to guide the stream but the further the edge was from her, the more unstable it became. The stream of power started to shudder and shake and the wind that surrounded her kicked up in urgency. Her hair whipped around her head and the wind pushed the desks loudly to the sides of the classroom. Several girls screamed.

Professor Kent was watching Eliza from the front of the classroom, a hungry expression on his face. Eliza was attempting to manipulate a force more powerful than she could control with no sign of giving up. A wand made light work of filling a glass but trying to control the element of water to move into a small vessel was no easy feat. Chaos reigned from her raw use of elemental magic and precisely illustrated the point Professor Kent was trying to make.

The water Eliza was trying to guide had just about reached the rim of the champagne flute. Every inch the power moved away from her, the harder it was to control. Her arms were vibrating painfully. Just as she thought she might be able to lower the water into the glass with success, she lost control and the crystal flute exploded. Shards burst outward like lethal swords in all directions. More screams escaped from her classmates.

"*Helaris!*" shouted Professor Kent, his wand pointed firmly to the exploding glass. The shards froze, suspended in midair. With a smug upward flick of his wand they disappeared.

"You may take your seat," said Professor Kent to a sweat-drenched and thoroughly exhausted Eliza. "As you all saw, performing magic with a wand is not only much easier to learn and control, but also far less destructive. Think of elemental magic as a bomb. Magic with a wand, or staff," he nodded in acknowledgement at the few warlocks who preferred staffs to wands, "is the scalpel. Far more precise. Far more elegant. A powerful warlock can produce powerful magic whichever he chooses to perform it."

Professor Kent paused as students pushed their desks back into their original positions. A few girls glared angrily at Eliza who was slumped exhaustedly in her seat. He addressed the class once more, "I know in your country you like to experiment with many kinds of magic. I've amused myself since arriving here by taking some of my colleagues' courses. I thought to improve my own knowledge of magic. But I must say, our school in England has been around for thousands of years and has focused mainly on Sorcery. There is something to be said, and respected, for time honoured traditions. We must not be fools who re-invent the wheel. The wisdom of our ancestors should guide us."

He gave a small smile to Eliza. "I hope that demonstration clarified why Sorcery, with a wand, is not only just as powerful but more versatile and useful that your so-called raw elemental magic."

Collapsed in her seat, Eliza did little to contradict the professor.

"What, um, sorry... I'm just wondering, you know... what are... um... what's your heritage?" Eliza asked Faye hesitantly one day. She could no longer pretend that the girl was human. She was so translucent as to sometimes cast doubt in Eliza's mind about her physically being in the room with them. And there was something otherworldly about her large black eyes.

The beautifully strange girl laughed, "Those types of questions can be a little sensitive."

"I'm sorry, you're just so... different. I was just

curious," said Eliza quickly, cheeks reddening. "Please pretend I didn't ask." She was kicking herself for being so tactless, but she hadn't been able to think of a better way to phrase the question.

"My father is a faery. My mother is a witch. I'm neither as far as I can tell," Faye paused as if considering her words carefully. "I'm cursed by my parents, really. I've inherited faery magic but it has mingled with witching magic in such a way that I can't control..." Eliza waited quietly for Faye to continue. "You see me here sitting with you at this table, but I exist simultaneously in another world. I move in both worlds and stay in neither. I've been trying to learn how to control it but... no luck yet."

"Wait—for real? You're in another world? Like another universe or something? Right now?"

Faye smiled shyly, "I feel like I'm constantly flickering between the two worlds like a badly tuned radio station. But it happens so fast it's not detectable in either world that I am leaving and reappearing dozens of times per minute. I hope I'll be able to find some form of magic that will allow me to move only when I choose. It started happening when I turned eight years old. I thought I was going crazy, seeing visions of a barren red planet. But my parents knew right away it wasn't visions. They could see I was sputtering out of existence like a candle going out. Then, I'd sputter back!"

"Can faeries travel at will between worlds?" asked Eliza. "Couldn't your dad teach you to control it?"

"That's the funny thing," said Faye, though there was no humour in her voice. "They used to be able to travel to other worlds beyond our own, but the knowledge was lost generations ago. They come from another realm, certainly. All the folk tales my dad's family tell, take place in landscapes that do not exist on this earth. How faeries came to arrive and stay here no one seems to know or remember."

Eliza was struck by the depth of this mystery. Her friend was sitting in front of her and was somewhere else entirely at the same time. It was mind boggling. She turned to Mashu, his squashed, furry face turned toward her in expectation.

"And... you...?" Eliza let the question hang in midair.

"My dad's a mop and my mom's a gorilla," he grunted in reply, spooning cereal into his mouth. Eliza and Faye sat with their mouths open, staring in horrified silence at Mashu.

He swallowed his cereal and his small beady eyes focused on their expressions. Suddenly he pounded the table with a furry white fist and started laughing hysterically.

"Aharharhar!" He guffawed. "Got you both good with that one, didn't I? Aharharharhar!"

Eliza and Faye exchanged a glance but said nothing. Mashu did not offer the real story and Eliza was not going to pry any more than she already had. They had fallen into a natural friendship based entirely on the fact that all three did not mix with the regular teenage students. Eliza felt too old and really had only come to live at the school to study. Faye was a few years older than her classmates, too, and said she didn't care for all the teenage talk of love and romance. As for Mashu, Eliza suspected he nursed a soft spot for Faye. She often caught him watching her with a gentle expression. None of them were in the same year as one another, but an unspoken agreement solidified between them that they would breakfast, lunch, and sup together.

By Samhainn, which was celebrated instead of Halloween in witching society, Eliza attracted the attention of one of her classmates. Melissa Sweet was enrolled in every single one of the same classes as Eliza. Each time they went to Herbalism, Melissa sat next to Eliza. Each time they slumped into the classroom for Energy Amplification (the study of magical tools), Melissa slid onto the bench next to Eliza. Transposition, Melissa was there. Sorcery, Melissa appeared. Elemental Magic, again, Melissa. Melissa was constantly offering Eliza tips and advice, and offering to study together after class in all the subjects Eliza struggled in. Which was most of them.

Eliza supposed she should welcome the help, but there was something repellant about the way Melissa Sweet was always so good-humoured and kind. It was nauseating how nice she could be. When Eliza continued to underperform in their Transposition class, Melissa would smile and say stupid things like "Practice makes perfect!" or "Rome wasn't built in a day!" These remarks might be meant to inspire, Eliza supposed, but when they were combined with the cheerful blonde's easy smile and the fact that she would immediately follow it up by performing the magic with impeccable perfection, it made Eliza's blood boil. Either Melissa was truly a nice person who was completely oblivious, or she was being purposefully patronizing. Either way, Eliza did not like her one bit.

Eliza arrived late to their Energy Amplification class, having completely lost track of time while trying to memorize the ever-increasing list of incantations she needed to perfect to be allowed to continue in her Sorcery class.

"Eliza!" called Melissa, beaming genuinely as Eliza entered the classroom. "Right here!"

Try though she might, Eliza never managed to protect herself from Melissa's intoxicating influence. She knew, of course, what was coming. She had tried to harden her heart when she entered the classroom with the complete intention of pretending not to see Melissa Sweet.

As always, however, Melissa was so bubbly and unabashedly *glad* to see Eliza that a toothy smile spread across Eliza's face against her will. Eliza wondered whether there was a magic to what Melissa did, but thought it more likely that her openness disarmed Eliza so much that the effect was entirely natural. Eliza found herself unable to reject the outgoing girl and made her way to the seat Melissa had saved for her.

"I was worried you weren't going to come!" whispered Melissa as the students all rustled to get their notes and tools organized for the lesson.

"How come?" asked Eliza, indifferently.

"Well, I don't know. I just know I would hate to see you give up just because you're struggling!"

Eliza stilled for a moment trying to decipher if this was meant as an insult or if this was just unfiltered truth.

"I've been doing much better in this class, though." Eliza responded in a low voice as Professor Stone entered the room. It was true, now in her fourth week she had finally caught up in the tool making class. She had memorized the uses of all the crystals they were presented and could identify them all correctly. She could recite the uses of different metals, and as of last week she knew all the different magical qualities of wood.

"Oh, I know," answered Melissa. "I've noticed that you're really amazing with physical magicks. It's more the intangibles that have you bothered, Transposition and Sorcery. But even then, you're really inspiring! It's not easy for you, but you try and you try and you don't give up!" Melissa smiled and Eliza wanted to punch her.

Eliza had certainly not intended for her lack of success to be a source of inspiration. It reminded her of a particularly painful memory. She had proudly strutted into high school wearing a tight new outfit. A friend of hers looked her up and down and said Eliza was so *brave* in an awestruck voice. Eliza never wore that outfit again. Squirming in her seat, Eliza prayed that Melissa had finished. She had not.

"It shows you're genuinely interested in the *process* of learning. Many people just focus on where they have natural talent and cruise through without ever pushing themselves." Thankfully, Eliza was spared having to respond to Melissa's assessment by the beginning of Professor Stone's lesson.

He was a large man, broad with rough hands and a weathered look about him. He always wore a brown leather apron over his clothes. The pockets of the apron were full of the tools one needed to work with stone, metal, and wood.

"All right, settle in. I expect you will all have memorized the fifteen woods that we primarily use in wand- and staff-making. You should also know their properties by now. I've had many a student become excellent at reciting the qualities that make oak a better choice for a broom, why yew makes a particularly powerful wand, and why poplar is a pitiful choice for a staff. However, the same student cannot pick maple out of a line-up. Today we'll be focusing on identifying the wood. It's all well knowing what something can do, but if you can't tell what wood you're using, a fat lot of good it will serve you when you decide to make something with it. I'll be passing samples around the room. Each sample has a number. You can work in teams today to figure out which is which." Professor Stone paused dramatically. "But be prepared that next week you will be tested alone and expected to identify these fifteen species of wood without help."

Melissa quickly invited the students from the surrounding benches to join them in identifying the woods. Eliza found these kinds of physical magicks to be straightforward. She identified eight of the fifteen samples for her classmates and together they figured out what the others were by process of elimination. Then, they spent a few minutes trying to notice differences in colour and grain to assist in identifying them the next time.

"You're really great at that!" complimented Melissa as they left the classroom to head to lunch. "Honestly, it all just looks like wood to me, you really got us going in the right direction!"

Eliza blushed and fought furiously with her

face. Her cheeks wanted to smile but Eliza was determined not to be charmed by Melissa. Grimacing, she said, "Identifying wood won't be much actual use in the real world. *You're* able to do all the spells we've covered so far in Sorcery. And I've noticed you using spells we haven't even covered yet when we're in the Grand Room. You would be much better in a duel."

Melissa laughed heartily, "I can't imagine why I would ever want to be in a duel, but you could identify the hardest type of wood and knock someone over the head with it while they're trying to think of a spell."

Laughter escaped Eliza before she could stop it.

"Want to have lunch with me and my friends?" Melissa invited. "We sit over there," and she pointed to a table of teens who were laughing raucously.

"That's really tempting," lied Eliza, "but I've already said I'd meet Faye and Mashu for lunch."

Melissa gave her a huge smile. "I thought you'd say that. I'll see you in class tomorrow!" and with that she bounded toward the other happy teens.

Eliza slid down onto a chair at the table where her friends would soon be meeting her and wondered why she needed to be so bitter and unhappy. She watched as bowls and cauldrons of soup floated out from the open kitchen doors, followed closely by baskets of bread rolls. None of the students present in the Grand Room gave any notice to this everyday display of magic.

These kids had their whole lives ahead of them, thought Eliza. Nobody looked at a woman nearly in her thirties whose only accomplishments were having an overgrown garden and an unusual friendship with a cat and thought "wow, she has a lot of potential." No, she thought bitterly. At her age there was no more *potential*. She was what she was and even if she learned to master all this magic she knew where she would end up in four years. Back in her house with her cat and her garden. Magic had arrived too late to change the course of her destiny.

"You look like crap," declared Mashu when he arrived. He sat next to her and grabbed a bread roll from a basket on the table before serving himself a bowl of leek and potato soup.

Faye lowered herself elegantly to her seat to join them, her presence shimmering insubstantially. "That's not a very nice thing to say, Mashu—"

"Thank you!" said Eliza.

"—even though it's completely true," finished Faye, to Eliza's dismay. "What happened this morning?"

Eliza darkly said, "I just had a class with Melissa Sweet." She shot a furtive glance over at the table where Melissa sat chatting with her friends.

Faye nodded, "And she outperformed you again?"

"No!" Eliza felt indignant.

"So, what's the problem?" grunted Mashu through spoonfuls of soup.

Eliza struggled to express what she felt. "It's like— it's like Melissa is living the life I wish I had. She's talented, pretty, and even though she is beautiful she isn't a horrible person. You can't be nice *and* pretty. You have to choose one or the other." Eliza said stubbornly.

"You're nice and pretty," said Faye and Mashu together.

A frustrated groan escaped Eliza. "I'm not fishing for compliments! I'm just trying to explain why I find her insufferable. And I'm not nice. I'm bitter and angry—almost all the time!"

Faye quietly took this in for a moment and said, "Maybe that is what it feels like to you, but I can promise you on the outside you're always very nice and charming. Melissa probably gravitates towards you for exactly that reason. Our friends are often reflections of the qualities we *like* in ourselves, and the people we hate are reflections of what we dislike about ourselves."

"Not to mention, if you hate Melissa for living the life you wish you had," interjected Mashu, "I hate to break it to you but you're both in the same school taking the same courses. You *are* living the same life. The only difference is you have a decade of disappointment under your belt while she still has that glowing '*anything is possible if you put your mind to it*' naivety." Mashu shrugged, "Maybe it's not such a bad thing. You could both learn from each other."

They ate the rest of their meal in silence, Faye frowning slightly over her meal. Mashu had three helpings of soup and Eliza pulled out her Transposition notebook from her bag and began trying to make a breadcrumb disappear.

"It would be much faster with a wand."

Eliza turned and found that Professor Kent was standing behind her, watching her progress.

"Yes, but that would be cheating. Transposition expects us to be able to make things disappear, appear, and travel *without* the use of a wand," answered Eliza, toeing the line between insolence and banter.

"I could teach you a spell that creates illusions. So you could give the *illusion* that you're doing this Transposition business properly, but beneath the illusion you would be waving a wand," suggested Professor Kent.

Faye, Mashu, and Eliza laughed. "You're encouraging cheating?"

"Isn't that what magic is? Cheating our way into a simpler life?"

Eliza reached down into her bag and pulled out a scroll that she released dramatically so the paper unrolled down to the floor. The scroll revealed the list of every spell Professor Kent had so far assigned as required material to pass the first exam. "You call *this* simple?" asked Eliza.

Professor Kent badly suppressed a smile. "Well, you will one day come to find my course is the only one that matters. You could learn to transport yourself with a wand, I don't see why you'd need to go through all this trouble with Transposition. You could cause happiness or pain with a wand, I don't see the point of making potions. You can control fire with a wand and yet I see from your calloused hands you've enrolled yourself into one of the silliest classes I've ever heard of—*Elemental Magic*."

"—Maybe just because you have difficulty learning these other kinds of magicks, doesn't mean they aren't as relevant." A tall, thin man with pale skin interrupted Professor Kent.

"Ah, Professor Claeg! How good of you to join us," said Professor Kent with the distinct air of not being happy to see Claeg at all.

"Which class do you teach?" asked Eliza.

"Necromancy," answered Faye, and the two professors in unison. A shiver ran down Eliza's spine. Professor Claeg wore tight black robes and had a dark goatee. His left ear wore a claw-shaped earring of what Eliza recognized as purple iolite.

"I teach students how to animate the corpses of

the dead. To communicate with lost spirits, and to control ghosts to do their bidding. Those who reach the highest level of my class can even conjure up the image and spirit of a person long deceased. Very few students have managed it, but it is my greatest pride when I see one accomplish it."

Professor Kent appeared at battle with himself but finally could not keep it in, "It is a foul, twisted, depraved, and might I add *prohibited* form of magic in most of the world. It is *shocking* to me that such dark magic would be *taught* in a school to *children.*"

A smile crept upon the side of Professor Claeg's mouth, and he seemed to grow taller as he responded. "A dog must first be taught to bark before he can be taught to be silent," he answered, bewilderingly. Professor Kent and Eliza shared a glance. Professor Claeg's attention was caught by this brief exchange of eye contact and focused upon Eliza, becoming noticeably shorter as he approached her. He leaned toward her and whispered close to her ear.

"Your mother says hi."

CHAPTER SEVEN
The Reading

Eliza's eyes widened and she felt her hands shake. Satisfied with this reaction, Professor Claeg stood tall and stalked away with a lopsided gait. Professor Kent stayed by their table, watching the other professor go while Mashu and Faye stared at Eliza. She felt shaky, her cat leapt onto her lap and she ran her fingers through his warm fur. "I'm—I'm gonna—I'm gonna go," she said. "I'll catch you guys later." And she dashed out of the hall holding Pal firmly in her arms, feeling his little heartbeat against her chest.

They ran out into the back courtyard and made their way to a little gazebo among the neatly clipped hedges. Eliza created a warm ball of flames to hover in front of them, keeping the chill of the November afternoon at bay. This was the second time the subject of Eliza's birth mother had come up this week. A few days earlier, in Sorcery, Professor Kent had also touched upon that long-buried subject.

Sorcery was one class that remained structurally

the same one week after the other. They would start by performing spells they had been assigned the previous week. Professor Kent would go around and correct their wand movements or their pronunciation of incantations. He would then send a new list of spells floating out around the class. The incantations, wand movements, and intentions were described as clearly on the page as possible. Students were expected to return to class the following week having memorized and learned to perform each of the spells. The punishment for not successfully achieving the list of spells during the week was an agonizing few minutes at the end of each lesson when Professor Kent would call out those students who needed to return to earlier spells and continue practicing.

"In addition to this week's assignment I would like Mr. Clemens to continue studying how to perform the light charm. You were barely able to cast a shadow with the amount of light you produced for us today. Miss Attiogbe, please give a little more attention to levitation. You'll notice no one else sent any objects crashing into the ceiling." He strolled haughtily up and down the rows of desks as he spoke.

"Miss Paladin. I'm sorry to say that listing the number of spells you have yet to master would take too much of your classmates' time. I expect students to achieve a great deal in a short amount of time and you began classes so late, you will have to continue to work very hard to catch up. After Christmas we will be doing much more advanced magic, as the basics should have been exhausted by then. It may be better if you drop this class and consider re-enrolling next year when you have more time to digest the material."

Eliza had been fuming. She knew that she might have taken on more than she bargained for by signing up for a full course load her first semester, despite arriving a month behind. Still, she felt it insensitive for her teacher to call her out in front of everyone. The week prior, he had already insulted her by saying "Miss Paladin, you have adequately performed repairing spells, lighting a flame, stirring a pot, and conjuring water. There is a list of fifty-six spells you have not yet mastered. You perform some of the magic, but with none of the finesse required to pass an exam. Please take the time to actually read the assignments and learn the incantations and wand movements. Stop trying to rely entirely on the intentions, which are where your strength lies."

Eliza, of course, had not been able to master fifty-six spells in addition to the ten new ones set for them that week. She decided it was time to admit she could not do it alone and ask for more help. The principal had told her when she arrived that this could be organized for her benefit. She approached Professor Kent at the end of class.

"Professor Kent. Can I have a word?"

"Ah! Miss Paladin!" he smiled warmly. "How can I help?"

"You seem weirdly happy to see me, considering you give the impression of hating me in class."

He raised an eyebrow at this. "I don't have the time or the energy to hate you! I imagine it must be very difficult for you, only now discovering you have magic and trying to keep up at this school. It's very fast-paced and very little time is spent nurturing students who are slower learners—" Eliza narrowed her eyes and balled her fists at this accusation. "I don't hate you. I just don't think you belong in my class."

"How can you say that? I can do the magic; I can perform the spells. I just haven't memorized every incantation yet!"

"Yes, which is why I suggested you leave my class and come back next year. This will give you the opportunity to master some of your other classes, which I hear you are also struggling in. And when you do come back, you will have had time to practice some of the first spells and be at the same level as our younger students. Perhaps your increased confidence from performing a dozen basic spells will allow you to progress at a better rate."

Eliza resisted the urge to stamp her feet in rage like a child. She gritted her teeth and held her tongue as he continued, "In my country there is a lot more *time* spent educating magical youth, and always from a young age. The idea that magic develops later in certain people is not part of the system in England. The mature students here at Kentree were a surprise to me. You simply cannot keep up to the younger students. There is no reason to feel shame."

Eliza was could no longer keep it in. "Can't you help me?" she demanded. "Instead of telling me to quit! I'm almost twenty years behind on my magical education—I don't want to delay another year!"

"It might surprise you to find out that I do have a life outside of the classroom," retorted Professor Kent. "I have my own projects I am working on. I don't feel particularly inclined to volunteer my time to a lost cause."

"Lost cause!"

"Yes, lost cause." Professor Kent now betrayed a note of impatience. "If you didn't have enough magic to register until you were—what, thirty?— I wonder why we are bothering. At this rate you won't be able to transfigure a twig into a stick by the time you're forty."

Eliza flushed and remained speechless.

"Listen," said Professor Kent, softening. "You've been excelling at all the physical branches of magic. Fire, water, earth, plants, magical tools (though you've yet to master wielding them). Why not dedicate yourself to those subjects, and leave the intangible magicks for those who were born with greater natural ability?"

Eliza clenched her jaw and bit back another retort. She had to remind herself that she had come to Professor Kent for help, and that she would not be so easily discouraged. "What are the other projects you are working on?" Eliza asked, attempting for a calm and polite voice. She had learned throughout her career that men were more easily swayed when they thought you were interested in their lives. They simply loved talking about themselves.

"Oh!" Professor Kent exclaimed joyfully. "Why, something rather close to the subject we are discussing! Where does magic come from? How does it manifest, why, and how is it measured? I tried to discover the answers to these mysteries in Britain, but I was dissatisfied with the lack of available information. But here, magic is seen from a totally different angle. I want to understand: how does Kentree measure the level of power in an individual?

"It has always been a fact that some spells require more power and skill than others, but before coming here I had never known anyone to be able to *measure* that data. Then, knowing that, we should be able to ask why some individuals have magic when others do not? Why some are more gifted, or powerful, than others? Why some Mundunces produce offspring capable of performing magic?"

Eliza's heart was still beating hard in her chest from the series of insults she had endured, but she tried hard to think of a follow-up question that would show both interest and flattery. Her nostrils flared and she settled for a simple, "And what have you discovered so far?"

At this, Professor Kent had a pained expression. "Principal Crinwere does not wish to share the magic used by Kentree to measure power, or to find students. Apparently, it could be dangerous in the wrong hands." A shadow crossed his face momentarily. "Magic is most common among those who come from magical families. Mundunces who create magical offspring are more rare, and I would love to determine what factors incite this. But the principal feels that the study is too political in nature to be of much academic use." He shot a hard look at Eliza which nearly threw her off balance. "Are your parents Mundunces?" he asked.

"I don't know," Eliza was stumped by the sudden question.

"A Mundunce is someone who has no magic," Professor Kent explained in a tone that might be used when speaking to a particularly stupid person.

"I was adopted," said Eliza. "I wouldn't know if my birth parents were magical or mundane, or whatever."

"I assume they must be. Mundunces." Professor Kent said curling his lip distastefully.

"What makes you assume that?" asked Eliza irritably, not liking his tone once again.

Wand twirling in his left hand, Professor Kent looked as though he relished in talking down to Eliza. "Your magic did not register for so long. Witches and warlocks from witching families usually display magic around eight years old. Thirty is unthinkable. If you were from a witching family in my country and not displaying magical ability until you were in your thirties you would long since have been encouraged to integrate with Mundunce society."

Eliza thought back to her conversation on her first day at Kentree and hesitated for a moment. It didn't seem enough that *she* knew that she had been magical all along. Despite Professor Kent being entirely frustrating, Eliza had a desire to prove herself worthy of inclusion. His barrage of insults ignited a desire to show him up.

"If I told you I have been performing magic for a lot longer, would you believe me?" asked Eliza, standing tall. "Someone tampered with my ability to use and see magic. They also put some kind of shield on me that prevented Kentree's ability to detect the times when I did break through the spells and managed to create my own magic. I remember causing incredible things to happen my whole life—ever since I was little!" Eliza was swept up in her own story, she was feeling excited again remembering how she had caused so many little mishaps at her school playground.

"Each time I made something fly, or once I parted the water in a pond when my cousin had fallen in—I wondered if I was part of something greater." Eliza leaned forward across the table conspiratorially. "Someone took that life from me. Someone took my magic and hid it. I couldn't even see faeries until after I got into the enchanted pool."

Professor Kent was looking at her as if he had found an incredible treasure. A mystery that needed solving was sitting in front of him. Eliza looked imploringly into his eyes. "I should have been here years ago. Holly told me. She said she only caught wind of me in September. But when Principal Crinwere consulted a crystal ball about my past, it was discovered that I had been performing powerful enough magic to attend this school since I was twelve! I ought to have been one of the youngest pupils ever to attend this school.

"Wasted potential," finished Eliza bitterly.

Silence stretched between the two for several long moments.

"Let me see if I understand, someone laid enchantments upon you from a young age to make it difficult for anyone to detect your magic?"

"Yes."

"Then, for good measure, they also tried to hide the magical world from *you*? That is to say, you could not see magic or understand that it existed?" asked Professor Kent.

With a pained shrug Eliza tried to explain, "More like I could only see as much as a—what did you call them? Mundane?"

"—Mun*dunce*."

"I could only see as much as a Mundunce could see. When I arrived here, I went into the enchanted pool in the school's gardens and suddenly I could see so much that had been hidden from me before."

Professor Kent nodded, interested. "They could not remove your magic, so they settled for hiding it from within and without... I wonder why they bothered. What could be gained from this? Only someone powerful could have pulled it off for so long..."

Eliza nodded, picking at a spot on the desk. "I can't understand why they would have wanted to take my power like that. They must have known I would be magical from when I was a baby."

"How did Kentree eventually discover you?"

"I started manifesting greater magic, with the help of my cat."

"Then you refused to give up your power. You

reclaimed what had always belonged to you and lo and behold your dreams came true." Professor Kent looked like an idea had occurred to him suddenly. "Have you enrolled yourself into fortune telling?"

"No, I've been reading runes for years. I get accurate readings, but I tend to ignore them when it isn't what I want to hear. Eventually I end up fulfilling the prophecy anyway, so it's kind of pointless. Knowing what's coming doesn't give me the ability to overcome it."

Professor Kent nodded and said, "You know you can use the runes to look backward as well as forward, don't you? The person who conjured the spells upon you may have protected themselves from detection from Seers, but as you are the subject in the event, you will be able to See what others cannot. When you consult on behalf of someone else, the collective unconscious may hide things from you that you do not deserve to know. If you ask a question about yourself, you are guaranteed an answer. You own your truth. The power of it cannot be taken or hidden from you forever."

Lost in thought at the prospect of finding out who had altered the path of her entire life, Eliza did not answer. It was not until Professor Kent spoke again that she remembered where she was or why she was there.

"Let's meet Saturday night after dinner in my classroom. It will be empty at that time. We can practice your wand work, then." He dismissed Eliza with a wave.

That night Eliza felt conflicted. She had achieved her goal of getting Professor Kent to help her with her wand work but found herself thinking about the mystery of her life for the first time since she started classes. She had been so busy proving herself that she had quite forgotten to wonder who had altered the course of her life—and why? The one thought that kept coming back to her was that her mother must be involved. Kent said it was far more likely to have magical abilities if one's parents were magical. Who else could have known Eliza would be a witch, if not her own mother? Eliza had not had time yesterday to read the runes, but she had dreamed of her mother when she tossed and turned last night.

Now, huddled with Pal in the cold courtyard, Eliza realized the meaning of Professor Claeg's words. *Your mother says hi.* This could only mean one thing; her biological mother was dead. Eliza ought to go up to her room immediately and pull out the runes to decipher her origin. She was not so sure she was ready to know. She left the courtyard, extinguishing her little fire by closing her fist, and made her way to her dorm room. Eliza stared at the ceiling for hours, knowing she should be studying but unable to think of anything except the confirmation that her birth mother was dead. She closed her eyes. When she opened them, the sun was rising and she had to prepare for another day.

After Transposition, Eliza's only class on a Friday, she had the whole weekend to enjoy. She sat in the Grand Room with Faye and Mashu for lunch. She knew she must not linger there too long today. She wanted to consult the runes and learn why she had been prevented from getting a magical education sooner. Nevertheless, Eliza enjoyed the company of her bizarre friends and indulged in the opportunity to learn more about the magical world.

Faye and Mashu provided a window into the society that she had not been allowed to join until now. She learned not to listen to a word of what Mashu said. He always preferred to make a joke over saying anything true. He had once told Eliza a great tale about how Kentree had been founded when the Witch Queen of the North slayed a dragon. The dragon's huge ribcage had been used as trusses to build the original school building. Then the Boulder People of the East (his ancestors, apparently) rolled in and easily shattered the building as the old bones had grown brittle.

"That's when Kentree bought this old church

compound," said Mashu, "they had the necromances conjure up such terrible spirits that the Mundunces who worshipped here ran away, tail between their legs! They sold the building and all the surrounding lands for pennies!"

Enraptured with the fantastic story, Eliza started a barrage of questions, "How big are dragons? Are there still dragons left? Where are the descendants of the Witch Queen now? Why would anyone build a church on an island in the middle of nowhere?"

Faye had let out a tinkling laugh, "Really Eliza, you shouldn't be so gullible! There is no royalty in the magical world, and I promise nothing from that story you just heard is true."

Faye was a real wealth of knowledge. She knew more about magical creatures than Eliza was sure even the teacher of Cooperation with Beings knew. Faye told Eliza about all the different creatures that lived in the little forest in the school gardens, what their nests looked like, which ones could perform magic and which ones were only considered magical because Mundunces could not see them. She also had a gift with air elements and entertained them with shimmering images made of tiny sparkling stars that she could conjure. Other students would turn to look, fascinated, at the marvelous illusions Faye created. She said she was making the veil between worlds transparent so that what they were seeing were not scenes from her imagination, but windows into other universes.

After lunch, Pal and Eliza made their way upstairs to their dorm room to retrieve the set of runes which was still in the small, velvet-lined trunk. Sitting on her bedroom rug, Eliza poured out the runes in front of them.

"You'll be assisting me with this, I assume," Eliza told Pal. "You know I'm too biased to properly do my own readings."

"Of course," replied Pal. "I wouldn't trust you to solve a mystery of this importance without me!"

Eliza spread the runes around in front of her. She asked her first question;

Who hid me from the magical world?

In answer, three runes pulsed energy into her palm and she turned them over. They were Othel, Ing, and Beorc.

"I wasn't expecting it to be this obvious who cast the spell," said Pal. Eliza could not disagree, even all the bias in the world could not confuse the meaning of these runes.

Eliza cried, "My own mother! It had to be, but it's crazy. Why deprive me of a magical life?" she wondered.

"Maybe she didn't like magic," suggested Pal. "We should ask the runes."

Eliza flipped the three runes over again so

that their symbols were hidden. She started a new reading, shuffling the stones in a clockwise fashion again and asked:

Why would my mother hide me from the magical world?"

This time it was much more difficult to choose the runes. In the end, she picked five from the spread and laid them before her and the cat. They were Thorn, Is, Tir, Eolh, and Rad in reversed position.

The meaning, again, was clear; conflict, inadvisable battle, protection, and travel. Her mother had been trying to protect her from dangers of her past. Of a past that took place in a land far away. Eliza had been hidden both magically and geographically. But why?

What happened to my mother, after she left me?

It was something she had long considered asking but never dared to. She gave the same advice to anyone who asked her to do a rune reading: do not to ask any questions to which you do not want the answer. After predicting the miscarriage of a long-awaited pregnancy, Eliza found she much preferred everyday questions— which college would accept you? Should you invest in this new company? Is it a good idea to plan a trip to Panama in December? None of these questions tended to destroy people's hopes and dreams.

One rune called her strongly. Two others followed. Her mother was captured. Imprisoned. Now dead.

She had received justice, according to the runes. She had been punished accordingly to her crimes. Eliza closed her eyes and felt through the runes to get in touch directly to the goddess which guided her. Understanding came to her. Her mother would have had to die nine deaths to receive equal punishment for what she had done. Her mother had even killed children.

CHAPTER EIGHT

Daughter of Evil

Pulling herself back from contact with the goddess, Eliza took a deep breath.

"Well, that's tough to come back from," Eliza exhaled. Pal waited patiently at her side for her to filter the information to him. "My mother was a murderer." Pal looked surprised at first but recovered quickly. He brushed himself heartily against Eliza's back in sympathy while she told him the rest.

"Your mother committed crimes and hid you here to protect you from the backlash of her actions?"

"That's what I'm interpreting, yeah," said Eliza. "She murdered nine people, and some of them were children."

Pal sat looking down at the runes. He pawed at the one that meant justice (Nied in reversed position), "She died in prison, that's sad."

"The goddess thinks it was just," shrugged Eliza, though it bothered her more than she cared to admit.

"Yes, well, what is clear is that your mother was not a very good person. I know you've often felt guilty for not mourning her."

Eliza chewed the edge of her lip before speaking, "I did feel guilty sometimes. In movies kids are always trying to find out *who they are* and for some reason they always think finding their birth parents will give them that. I've thought about my birth parents, sure, but I've never thought about their identity defining *me* in any way." She sat quietly for a moment, "Maybe I didn't mourn her enough, but now I'm damned if I do and damned if I don't."

Pal's tail flicked lightly, "Your birth mother's identity does define you. She was a witch and so are you. Her being a murderer has defined your whole life: where you grew up, with who, and not knowing what you were capable of. But it doesn't have to affect who you become. You can choose who you want to be."

"She was clearly deranged," Eliza felt more disconnected from her birth mother than she ever had before. "I wish I could go back to not knowing anything about her."

Pal head bumped her thigh affectionately, "Not so deranged that she didn't think to protect you. She journeyed all the way here, put protection spells on you and left you with a Mundunce family to live a life outside of magical society. Say what you will about your mother, but she cared about you. Imagine if she had let you grow up among the families of her victims. Who would trust you? Who might decide to take their revenge out on you?"

Eliza stroked the cat. "I wonder who she was," she whispered, "I wonder who she hurt, and why."

"Do you really want to know?" asked the cat.

"Not knowing my whole life didn't help much. Everything leading up to today has been directly affected by things that happened before I was even born. I've been entirely shaped by decisions that were made without me even being conscious. I'm from somewhere else, living here because someone decided it should be so. I want to know, so I can understand why I was treated like a Mundunce for twenty-eight years! Twenty-eight years of feeling like I could be something more, *do* more. But I couldn't, I was shielded from what my heart felt was possible. All because *my mother* decided that I should miserably sell my hours in a nine to five with Mundunces rather than live a life of danger and prejudice."

"You disagree?" asked Pal.

"Prejudice and danger sound a lot more fun, to be honest," Eliza started to laugh. It was a nervous sort of laugh. She knew there was nothing funny about what she'd learned but the tension and frustration needed to be released and laughing about murders and judgement helped a little.

Saturday broke foggy, and Eliza was unsure whether she should tell anyone what she learned about her mother. She was meeting with Professor Kent that evening and wondered if he would ask whether she had looked into her past. It was, after all, part of the reason he agreed to give her a private lesson. As the hours to supper passed, she ran over various scenarios in her mind. She could tell the complete truth, of course. She could lie and make up a whole new version of events. Or she could give him just enough true information to satiate his interest and no more. After all, he was only interested to know if she had witching folk as parents instead of Mundunces. None of the rest mattered, surely? At least not to him.

Mashu and Faye chit chatted while they ate and did not press Eliza to join in the dinner conversation. There was an unspoken understanding among the three friends. Often it was either Faye or Mashu who were wrapped up in their studies for a few days at a time. Both were in higher grades than Eliza, and their studies were even more grueling than hers. Since Eliza was always busy trying to catch up with her coursework, this suited her perfectly.

Eliza kept her eye on a long table where the staff usually ate together. She saw Professor

Kent in conversation with Principal Crinwere. The principal never disappointed in clothing choices. Sometimes they wore pinstriped suits with their hair short and slicked back. Other days they wore silk gowns with cascades of golden curls falling down their back. Eliza enjoyed the extravagance. Today, Principal Crinwere wore a deep shade of lipstick and a midnight blue jumpsuit. Hair in a complicated up-do, Principal Crinwere was the definition of femininity. But when the principal dressed in masculine clothes, the effect looked just as good. Eliza smiled at the confidence, hoping she could be as unashamedly true to herself someday.

When supper was over and Eliza saw Professor Kent slipping out of the Grand Room, she bade her friends a good evening and followed him out. Faye and Mashu exchanged looks of mild surprise; usually the three remained seated at their table and studied together until the late hours of the night.

Eliza knocked on Kent's classroom door, she knew she was not prepared to practice almost seventy spells. The Latin and Greek were confusing and difficult to pronounce. Her brain was not as elastic as the brains of her teenage classmates. She was having to learn a whole new language while trying to do complicated wand movements *and* focusing on her intentions. Regret prickled as she remembered insisting that she would not give up this branch of magic. For a wild moment Eliza considered running in the other direction before Professor Kent could answer the door.

"Come in," he said. "How are you this evening?"

Eliza grimaced.

"From your tortured expression, I gather you are still bothered by Professor Claeg's comment to you yesterday. Did you know your mother was dead?" Professor Kent's tone was kind.

"No, I didn't know," said Eliza. "Like I told you, I was adopted. I never knew my birth mother, but I didn't know she was dead…"

Silence hung between them for a few moments, and Professor Kent asked whether Eliza had the opportunity to investigate why she had been hidden from the magical world. Throat tightening, Eliza answered, "My mother was a witch. She wasn't from here; she came from another country. She brought me here to protect me from… I'm not sure. She cast spells to protect me from whatever she was running from. Then she went back to where she came from and… and died." Eliza carefully omitted the part about murder. She wasn't sure if she wanted to go there yet.

"I see, and your father?"

"Oh, I completely forgot about him." Eliza realized with a jolt. "I guess I've always assumed the man who was my biological father might not even have known my mother was pregnant."

"Maybe you should find out," said Professor Kent. "It might drastically change the story you are telling yourself about your past."

Eliza hesitated, "I think I could find out who my mother was, if I knew where she was from. I got the feeling she was well-known."

Professor Kent nodded. "Well, it would be interesting to know why she would have had to hide you. Given your age, she may have been involved in a sticky witching war that broke out in Britain, Europe and parts of Africa. The conflict lasted a few years and would have been coming to an end around the time you were born."

"There was a war twenty-eight years ago?"

"Yes…More like thirty years ago. But like I say, it lasted a few years and then it took several more years to capture all the criminals. Some of those who weren't caught still show up now and again. Just to remind the world they exist."

"What was the war about?" Eliza asked. "Why would witching folk fight amongst themselves?"

The professor perched himself on the edge of a desk, "It was about who should be allowed to wield magic, interestingly enough. The thought was that some people were more worthy than others to use it. In Britain, magic is almost entirely taught using wands. One side began removing wands from those they did not deem worthy and controlled production. Those who had grown up and been trained only ever to produce magic with a wand felt utterly powerless without them."

Eliza interjected, "Couldn't they just make their own wands?" She was thinking of Energy Amplification and her own growing collection of handmade wands.

"We did not have such a course at the school I attended. Wand making is an art very few ever learn in Britain. Without their wands, people could not perform even the simplest spell. The magic here, at this school, baffled me when I first arrived. How can my entire magical education be boiled down to just one subject among a dozen others? How could there be so many ways to produce magic without this thin, easily breakable piece of wood in my hand?" Professor Kent chuckled to himself. "Unfortunately, my family's side lost. I was only a toddler then. Everyone who had lost their wands were given new ones, and those who had killed Mundunce mutts were sent to prison for their crimes. My parents hadn't involved themselves with actual fighting, thank goodness. They just provided financial support. Having a toddler at home was a good excuse for them not to get blood on their hands."

Eliza ruminated on this information too, "So," she began, "in Britain people are powerless without wands. And one side wanted to take power from those they thought were unworthy. How did they decide? Is it like here, with the levels of power?"

"No, no, no. I told you last time, in Britain we do not have the concept of measuring power as they do here at Kentree. It had to do entirely with the family to whom you belong. Mix your family line with a Mundunce, for instance, and you and any offspring of that union would be considered unworthy by the side that incited the most violence."

"Your family were on the losing side; they wanted to take power from the mixed families?" Eliza was struggling to understand. "Why would someone become unworthy of having magic by marrying a Mundunce? Or having a kid with one?"

"Don't get me wrong, my family does not hate Mundunces. We *need* them. We have amassed our modest fortune by using magic to help Mundunces. We accomplish wonders for them and in return we have been afforded wealth, land, and even some titles. It is in our family's interest that there be a population of people who cannot perform magic, that we may appear all the more powerful. I, for instance, was not a terribly good student at my school. But by moving to this continent, where no one was well-versed in Sorcery, there was an opportunity for me. Here, I am a big fish in a small pond. No one bothers to question whether I am entirely qualified to be a professor simply because of where I grew up. My school specialized in Sorcery. I have more knowledge and resources about this subject than anyone else in North America. Though my family may be entirely mediocre at magic, we prefer to distinguish ourselves from and place ourselves above those who have none.

"Why would we want to share a gift with other people, if it could be prevented?"

Eliza's heart was racing. Maybe her mother had conceived Eliza with a Mundunce. Maybe Eliza was mixed. This could explain why her mother had to hide her far from the war. And the enchantments that hid her magical ability would be because she knew there would be people who disapproved of her parentage. Maybe she had killed nine people in self-defense.

"The good side won, though," said Eliza.

"Those who believe in equal access to all won. Those who championed segregation lost."

This stopped Eliza's hopes short. If her mother returned to the war after leaving her baby, and had been captured and imprisoned, it seemed likely she was a criminal after all. Surely the runes would not say she received her just desserts if her mother had only killed people in defense of her child. But then Eliza remembered her mother had also killed children. There did not seem to be a redemptive explanation possible for such an act.

Now Eliza had to face a new possibility. She was not just the child of a murderer, but the child of a bigot. Her mother might have believed in this classist ideology and fought to keep magic from people she deemed unworthy. "So... your family would condone the murder of innocent people?" Eliza asked, trying for a casual voice.

"Is anyone innocent during a war? Soldiers are usually celebrated, not accused of murder," there was a definite edge in Kent's voice.

With a dismissive wave of her hand, Eliza pressed, "You think it would be okay to murder someone because they were born from a non-magic family, and somehow had the ability to produce magic?"

Professor Kent drew himself up to full height. "All is fair in war, is it not?"

Eliza nodded, thinking that she needed to consult the runes again, to confirm if her mother had really been involved in this war. At least she knew now that Kent would not treat her differently if he found out her mother had been a murderous criminal. He was all for it.

"Witching folk are superior to ordinary people. In time, when you begin to see the full potential of what you are capable of, you will not want those powers taken from you again. You will not want to share those gifts with runts from a litter of Mundunces who have stumbled accidentally onto something that belongs to you."

"My father might have been a Mundunce... if he was, would you think I deserve to have my magic taken from me?" offered Eliza, wanting to hear it contradicted.

"Oh yes," said Professor Kent without hesitating. "Yes, I would have thought that was obvious."

They stood in silence for a few seconds, then—

"Shall we begin with the shrinking spell?"

CHAPTER NINE
The Lost Talisman

Tuesday Eliza had Elemental Magic. She had greatly improved in this class over the course of the semester. The students had spent the last few months working with the element of Fire. They conjured flames in the palms of their hands and each week learned techniques to fine tune the magic that could be accessed by producing fire. The month before Eliza started, students had already covered creating warmth, conjuring a flame, making the flame dimmer or brighter, increasing or decreasing the heat intensity and producing blue and green flames. Then, wisely, they learned how to put out a fire.

In the weeks since Eliza joined the class, she studiously caught up to her classmates and continued to learn new skills, such as creating a fireball and throwing it at a target or creating a stream of fire that could be dragged around the body into a steady ring of fire around oneself.

"This is particularly useful since dark creatures

and animated corpses can be kept safely at a distance using this magic. Since we teach necromancy at this school, I think it's good to also teach you to combat the pawns of the puppeteer," explained the teacher, Professor Soother, with a smile.

This week, they were using the power of flame to brand wood. It was a little tricky. At first, they were to use their hand to burn a handprint onto a plank of wood. The students were told they would eventually progress to creating a simple design and branding the wood from a distance. Eliza could not fathom that they would be able to cover all this in just one lesson. Her and all her classmates were already struggling. They could call forth the fire to brand the wood with their hand, but not without accidentally lighting the plank on fire. They were outside in the gardens, having had to leave the classroom when it was time to play with fire.

"By the time the cold really sets in this winter, we should have moved past the basics of raw flame and progressed into the finer points of fire magic that will not cause so many bangs and smoke," called out Professor Soother. She was a beautiful woman, perhaps in her fifties, built like a weightlifter. She had thick upper arms and a slim waist. Strong though she appeared, she was also sweet and understanding. Eliza wondered whether it was her own natural talent with fire, or a commentary on Professor Soother's excellent teaching that meant that she and her fellow students rarely had to do any extra homework after one of these lessons.

"Shoot." Eliza tutted, as once again her hand contacted the wood and immediately caused the plank to burst into flame. Professor Soother was wandering between them all, watching as they made their attempts. Eliza tried again, thinking this time if she warmed her hand and only touched the wood briefly, whipping her hand away before the plank could catch fire, she might be successful. For a second, she really thought she had it, but with a gasp of pain, she looked down at her hand and found it entirely covered in angry red blisters that pulsed painfully. The wood had a black imprint of her hand, but even this was glowing red with embers—something they were told did not count as a success.

Hearing Eliza cry out in pain, Professor Soother approached and took Eliza's hand into her own. Eliza's hand looked tiny and fragile in Professor Soother's large, rough one. Eliza winced when the professor raised a finger toward the blistered palm, but her touch was gentle. Professor Soother's whispered words were whisked away in the wind and Eliza felt the pain drain away. The professor's finger traced the palm of Eliza's hand gently. Eliza looked down to see what Professor Soother had done. The palm was not as it had been before, pink and smooth, but bore the scars of many healed blisters. It was rough but completely painless.

"Thank you," Eliza said, breathless.

Professor Soother did not answer but held her arms up to capture the attention of the rest of the class.

"You are all forgetting everything we have done leading up to this day. Do you think it is a coincidence that we are doing this now, and not before any of our previous lessons? You need the power to increase or decrease the intensity of the fire, you need to produce heat without flame, you must control the fire so that when you touch the wood you can snuff out its attempt at kindling. You must *combine* all that I have taught you. And remember—we do not concentrate heat in our hands, we are merely conductors! Allow the energy to flow through you, do not allow it to build up with no release. Again!"

This time students advanced more quickly. Eliza focused not on her hand but on the wood beneath it and called forth a light steady heat. She increased it until she saw the handprint beginning to appear in the wood and then she called the magic back out from the plank to prevent it from catching. There it was; a perfect impression of her hand.

By the end of the lesson, they had all successfully decorated wooden boards with smiling faces, images of animals, their own names, and whatever symbols they were able to imagine. There were a lot of excited voices talking loudly as they made their way back inside. So much so that Professor Kent popped his head out of a classroom and asked for the Elemental Magic group to "Please remember you are in a *school* not a playground!"

"Why even bother teaching her?"

Eliza overheard some students whispering over breakfast one December morning. "Imagine being so unmagical that you don't manifest until you're life is halfway over. If it were me, I would've been too embarrassed to come."

The group of students started laughing cruelly but the laughter turned to a shriek as the speaker began to shrink quickly down to the size of a marble.

"Well done," said Professor Kent, who Eliza realized with a jolt had been standing right behind her. "Shrinking something as complicated as a mammal is quite advanced—more than what we worked on the other night. I'm impressed," Eliza blushed at being caught red-handed. Professor Kent looked smart in a navy two-piece suit. "However, using magic on other students is not permitted within the walls of Kentree." He considered Eliza with a calculating expression.

"Give me your wand," he said.

Eliza looked at Professor Kent's extended hand in indignation. "My wand? What for?"

"As we discussed, depriving you of your wand is a tactic some may use to strip you of power. Power you clearly should not be trusted with," he indicated the tiny student who was crying and begging for someone to make her big again. "I happen to know you've carved several wands now in your Energy Amplification course, so you'll have to practice with one of those until your next class with me."

Eliza gave Professor Kent her wand reluctantly and glared as he walked away.

"That's so unfair! He knows I suck at wand magic, and now I won't be able to practice properly before next week's lesson. As if I have time to break in a new wand. I'm *still* behind in three of my six subjects!"

Faye was on a completely different thought. "You two look like you should be a couple."

Eliza was taken aback, "—what?"

With a playful smile Faye poked at Eliza, "It's just that you're both attractive, you have similar features and you're around the same age. You guys look like a matching pair," Faye's giggle was so infectious Eliza joined in.

Eliza considered this for a moment. Professor

Kent's head was blessed with thick hair, and a pronounced brow ridge. His lips were neither thin, nor plump, but had a gentle downward curve. When he had occasion to smile, his front teeth competed for space but the effect was charming. He was certainly not handsome by the standards of Hollywood leading actors. Still, Eliza had to admit there was a certain quality about him that was very appealing.

"I guess he's good-looking… but I resist the idea that I should be into someone just because they're my age and sort of look like me!"

"You're right," said Faye, laughing. "It's a cliché. Couples often look so much like one another they could be related!" Eliza tossed a piece of bread in Faye's direction. "But combine that confident swagger, the English accent, and an age-appropriate school-teacher fantasy and I think you could find other reasons to like him."

There were just two weeks left before Yule holidays. Eliza made her way through the manicured gardens, hugging Pal warmly against her chest. She was wearing a large woolen cloak over her clothes and a warm knitted hat on her head. She headed toward the forest. It was a chilly day in December, her breath fogged in front of her, and frost kissed the grass. She loved when the seasons produced special little moments of beauty. Like when the first flowers of spring appear, or when the trees turn orange in fall, or when snow glitters like a million diamonds on a sunny winter day. Despite the cold, Eliza wanted to enjoy the first hard frost of winter. The branches of all the trees were painted white with the finest icicles of moisture.

She was about to settle herself on a bench at the edge of the forest when a figure appeared bursting suddenly from the trees.

"Ah!" yelled Eliza, dropping Pal. The cat landed on four paws and hissed at the person that had just appeared stumbling out toward them.

"S—sorry!" It was Patty, the girl with whom Eliza had supper her first day at Kentree. "I've just—you haven't seen my t-talisman, have you? It's about this size." Patty made a circle with her hands indicating a large round object. "It has a jade in the c-center and the metal is forged into the shape of roses."

It took a moment for Eliza to register the words, she was startled at the state of the girl. Soaked through her clothes, hair clinging wetly to her cheeks, and the tips of her hair turning white with frost. Patty's cheeks were flushed red from the cold, but her eyes burned in desperation.

"Eliza?" prompted the girl, shivering and blue in the lips.

"No, I haven't seen a talisman. Why? Is it important?" Eliza was bewildered. Surely getting warm and dry ought to be Patty's priority.

"I m-made it in my first year of Energy Amplification, y-you know, the class where people make wands and s-staffs and things."

"Yes, I'm taking it this year."

"R-right, well, the th-thing is I've created all my s-spells with it ever since I made it." Patty's teeth chattered from cold, "It's like a bond. It's b-become a part of me. And it's learned f-from me as well. I've been t-trying to recreate the magic I did w-with it with another amulet I made but it's s-sluggish and s-stupid. Like starting from scratch again." Tears streamed down the girl's face. "I feel like I've lost my arm."

Eliza understood. It was no picnic casting spells with a new wand. She learned this the hard way and was relieved when Kent gave her back her precious first wand after only a few days. She smiled kindly at Patty, "We can sort this out quickly. Do you know how to do a summoning spell? Or we can do divination and ask the Goddess to tell us where it is. Or—"

Patty cut her off, "I've b-*been* trying. I've had three teachers t-try to summon it for me, I've asked my friends to look through a c-crystal ball, tea leaves, tarot, I've even b-been to the enchanted p-pool to see if maybe s-someone had erased my m-memory of its location. Nothing! It's v-vanished and I don't know how to do m-magic without it."

This was why the girl was soaking wet. She had been to the enchanted pool, and when that proved unsuccessful, she found herself freezing and unable to perform the magic she needed to dry herself. Eliza closed her eyes and used her hands to direct what heat she could find in the earth toward Patty. Eliza encouraged the moisture that soaked Patty's hair and clothes to dissipate into the air. In just a few seconds, it was done, and Patty was warm and dry (though Eliza regretted that Patty's hair now looked like a wild bird's nest and made a mental note to refine her technique before attempting the spell again).

This display of magic did not do much to improve the girls' spirits; Patty started sobbing loudly. Eliza reached an arm around Patty's shoulders and accompanied her back into the center cathedral.

"I think the best thing if you're having trouble with your magic is to have a good rest. It might just be the stress and worry of losing your talisman," Eliza suggested, "you just need to recenter yourself."

Patty wiped a tear hastily from her eye and glared at Eliza, "Don't act like you know anything," the girl spat venomously. "You think after five minutes you know more about it than I do! It's been missing for four days. I didn't even worry about it the first day, I knew I could *theoretically* do the same magic with a wand, or a staff, or even another talisman. But that's the thing. By day two I realized I couldn't do *any* magic. I'm impotent!"

Patty threw Eliza a dirty glance and launched herself down the hall, the long purple winter cloak she wore billowed behind her. Reflecting on this peculiar incident, Eliza decided she ought to discuss it with her friends at supper. Perhaps they had heard of someone losing an object and consequently losing their powers.

It sounded like what Professor Kent had told her about taking away people's wands. It wasn't exactly the same. Patty was sure to have learned how to perform magic without her talisman. The talisman would only have assisted in enhancing her natural power, so losing it should not have meant she would also lose her abilities. Eliza had still been able to perform magic with her other wands, albeit not as well.

Eliza arrived in the Grand Room too early for supper, eager as she was to discuss the day's events. Since neither Faye nor Mashu were presently in attendance, Eliza decided to use her time wisely. She tried to study her notes on the effects of combining different metals for Energy Amplification, but couldn't focus. Finally, supper arrived on plates that floated out of the open kitchen doors and drifted to each table. It was with delight that the smell of steak and mushroom pie reached Eliza. She had already started eating when Mashu and Faye appeared, following the seductive scent of the evening meal.

Eliza wasted no time telling them about her peculiar run-in with Patty. Mashu didn't seem surprised. "She's in my year. 'Been struggling the last few days. Keeps crying in class and can't even make a ball of fire anymore," Mashu snorted. Fire, Eliza had learned, was the elemental magic that was easiest to learn. "She hasn't even been able to do any simple charms. Professors think it's a mental block but she's being very dramatic about it. Like someone could have done this to her on purpose."

"What do you mean, on purpose?" asked Faye quickly.

Mashu looked uncomfortable as he glanced at Faye from beneath his thick brow, "She, um, she is starting to think she was targeted by someone... that someone took her magical ability."

"Could that happen?" asked Eliza in a panic. She had just discovered her wonderful abilities and was loath to see them taken away.

Faye chuckled, "I doubt it. People would have done it by now if it was possible," Faye put her fork down gently before continuing. "There are lots of stories about people no longer being able to use magic, but the general consensus is that it's caused by an emotional shock, or trauma. They become like Mundunces. Regular people, and integrate into Mundunce society."

Mashu was picking at his mashed potatoes feigning disinterest in the subject, but Eliza could see his body was tense as he listened.

"Caused by emotional shock? You could forget how to use magic because of a shock?"

Faye sighed dramatically, "I wish I knew more, but it's poorly documented. When witching folk lose their magic, they are embarrassed to admit it. Or their families hush it up."

"But this girl was seriously good at magic one day," interjected Mashu, apparently unable to help himself. "and the next— poof. No more magic. She came into class as happy as ever, clinging to her boyfriend and giggling. It wasn't until we started changing water into gin that she realized anything was wrong. She had no trauma when she walked in!"

Faye's lips curled in a smile, "None that *you* know of."

Eliza seized the opportunity to voice her own concerns. "I don't like the sound of this," she said. "Someone blocked my magical abilities for most of my life—how would it be if after all this hard work and discovery, one day you can't do the *one* thing that makes you special?"

Faye dismissed this quickly, "It's different, you

had magic all along, and it sounds like you were manifesting it frequently enough. Someone just put some spells on you to keep you out of the magical world."

"But I could lose it again," said Eliza.

Faye appeared conflicted. "I—I mean, what if she is no longer a witch? What if the magic went away, and she will never recover it? Would that be so bad?"

Eliza cried out, "Bad? It would be the worst possible outcome! How could you ask such a thing?"

"Magic isn't always a gift, Eliza," replied Faye drily.

Mashu and Eliza looked at one another uncomfortably. "Is that what *you* would want?" asked Eliza. "Have you been considering removing your magic entirely as a solution to your flickering problem?"

Faye answered, "It would be nice just to exist in one world without watching my back in the other."

"Is this something you've looked into?"

"I wish. I wrote a thesis proposal last year hoping I would be allowed to study the possibility of removing magic. But Principal Crinwere called me in to tell me they didn't approve of such research. They also said it could too easily be used for nefarious purposes if it was determined to be possible."

"Did you ever find anything that suggested it could be possible?" asked Eliza, worriedly.

"No, of course not! I wasn't given access to materials that would assist in my research," there was a touch of indignation in Faye's tone.

Mashu glanced up from a mushroom he had just stabbed with a fork, "That alone would stop you from trying?"

It was with a bright sparkle in her eye that Faye answered, leaning forward enthusiastically in her seat. "Obviously my research is focused on the sole intent to help *me*. But anyone else whose magic controls them could benefit from this sort of breakthrough!" Her voice was lowered to a whisper, "I've heard of some kids whose magic gets so pent up and out of control they literally explode! Imagine saving lives by removing magic!"

Mashu (who had heard this before) and Eliza were not much inclined to agree with Faye. The meal ended in silence, and none of them lingered long after. Eliza retired to her room and made a silent prayer of thanks to the Lunar Goddess for the powers she had been gifted before spending a few hours studying by a light she conjured from the palm of her hand.

CHAPTER TEN
The Necklace

When Eliza went into Transposition the next day, Melissa Sweet took the place next to her. Eliza braced herself for the irritatingly cheerful "Good morning!" with which Melissa usually greeted her. It was a surprise, therefore, to hear nothing but a thump as Melissa fell into her seat.

"Hey, are you OK?" asked Eliza, in spite of herself.

Melissa appeared surprised to see her. "Oh yes, thank you. I've just lost something that was special to me. I'm sure it'll turn up though…"

Eliza's eyebrows shot up. "Something important to you… something you used to create magic?"

Melissa appeared to be hearing her from far away. "Oh no, nothing like that. Just a necklace I've had since I was little. It was my great-grandmother's. I've never taken it off." She gazed at the stained-glass window while her finger played around the hollow of her neck.

"How did you lose it if you never take it off?"

"That's the thing that worries me," murmured Melissa. Professor Neach entered the room and the class settled down. "I know I had it on when I went to bed last night. But when I woke up this morning—it was gone. I pulled off my sheets and my pillowcase and searched everywhere but it's not in my room." She looked at Eliza with watery eyes, "Someone took it from my neck while I was asleep," Melissa whispered fearfully.

A shiver went down Eliza's spine. Two lost objects in as many days. But what purpose could someone have of a talisman and a necklace?

The girls were silent for the rest of the lesson. This week's session involved focus and attention. They were learning to move objects from one side of the room to the other, with increasing difficulty. Melissa was usually more adept at this type of magic, but today Eliza had progressed to moving a tray complete with teacups, saucers, and a teapot filled with hot water through the air using only the focus of her mind. Meanwhile, Melissa had not even managed to send an inflated balloon across the room. The balloon did travel a few feet toward the other end of the classroom by the end of the lesson, but Eliza was sure she saw Melissa give it a hard flick.

As they were packing up, Eliza grasped Melissa's shoulder firmly in what she hoped was an encouraging way. It was with heavy heart that she left Melissa in the classroom where she continued to frown in concentration at the balloon which bounced tauntingly on the classroom floor.

Eliza was dodging her way through a crowd of students gathered by the exit and accidentally walked straight into a tall, broad back. "Eliza," said Professor Kent, looking around in surprise.

"Sorry, I got jostled by the crowd."

"Not to worry, I was wanting a word with you anyway," he said good naturedly. "I wondered whether you've managed to identify your parents, or have you lost interest in that particular hobby?"

Eliza hesitated for a moment, then gestured Professor Kent to follow her into an empty classroom.

"The thing is, I'm not sure how much I'm really prepared to know. The other night, well, I thought I did want to find out who my mother was, and who my father is, but... I can't bring myself to ask any more questions. The little I discovered the one time I asked was enough to make me wish I had never been curious in the first place."

Professor Kent leaned in conspiratorially. "Did you leave something out of the story you told me?"

"My mother... she... the runes said she killed people."

Professor Kent's eyebrows rose in surprise.

"Including children," added Eliza bitterly.

"We have to find out who she was," he said excitedly.

"Why?" Eliza asked. Her whole life she'd been deprived of magic and the desperate desire to find out *why* had evaporated almost as soon as she had found out it was because of her birth mother. "Why would I want to know anything about those people? Why would I want to be associated with a murderer who left me in a society where I didn't belong?"

"You wanted to know why you'd been hidden from the magical world. Your parents were protecting you from their own reputation! Imagine going to school with children and teachers who every time they looked at you, they hated you because your mother killed a family member—an aunt, a mother, a sister. Your parents sent you away from all of that unfair judgement."

There was a long pause. Eliza was staring at her shoes, unable to bring herself to find interest in her parent's plight. "They were likely in our war," Kent said softly, "We might have been classmates had they not sent you to live in a family of Mundunces on the other side of the world."

"You're assuming an awful lot," argued Eliza, defiantly meeting his dark brown eyes, "I might be from a million other places in the world."

Professor Kent modestly agreed, "Well yes, perhaps I am seeing things that would fit a narrative I find convenient. But the timeline works. My parents, funding the war effort, your parents fighting in the front lines. Your mother slays a few people, finds out she's pregnant. The war is lost, and she knows the families of her victims will stop at nothing until they find her. She runs away to have you in a country where no one will ask where this strange little witch came from and leaves you here."

There was another pause and this time Eliza held Kent's gaze. She felt her cheeks warm, and she returned her eyes to the floor. "But I haven't even told you everything yet," she said. With a shaky breath, Eliza gathered the courage to say out loud the damning judgement the Gods had given her mother. "She was caught. She was imprisoned and died in confinement. The runes called it *justice*."

Eyes widening, Kent failed to hide a look of admiration, "I'm so sorry for your loss," he said, quickly rearranging his features to convey sorrow. "But... it fits with my theory! You see, she was captured for her crimes. She was one of us, on the losing side! Fighting to keep out unworthy Mundunce offspring from knowing and appropriating our ways" he rejoiced. "There can be no doubt about your blood purity, your father must have been a warlock, too!"

"Stop!" cried Eliza. "Why would I want to be part of a group of people who think it's right to deprive others of what their very *soul* most needs? I knew

I must be magical, I knew I must be special, but the world constantly reminded me of how mediocre and *ordinary* I was. Life was nothing to be celebrated, just an endless boring slog. Why would anyone *ever* want to condemn someone to that sort of life?"

"But don't you see! You, more than anyone should know some people don't *deserve* to be part of the magical world. Not everyone is worthy of our secrets. Surely you must see around you that some of these children are so pathetically ordinary that despite being able to light a fire with a wave and teleport a teacup to the kitchen sink, they have no true imagination like what it would take to reshape the world. Magic is meant to impact, improve, and alter. What purpose would there be if it weren't for creating true change?"

"We can't know that Chad the Mediocre won't grow up to be an incredibly powerful Wizard. It isn't for us to decide."

"He could," conceded professor Kent, "but what would he do, as a powerful Wizard? There are doers and dreamers, and then there is the vast majority of people who are simply administrators. I will be the first to admit, I scoffed at your desire to learn magic. You're only a few years younger than me and you're an entire career behind, I mean, why bother? But then I saw your drive, your determination. You were thoroughly humiliated day after day by all of your much younger classmates outperforming you in every subject—" Eliza fought the urge to strike him in the face "— and even so, you continued to work hard. I can see it in your face when you try and try again. Despite the fact a spell is working for *everyone* else in the room, you have this instinct inside you telling you *'don't quit, you're better than everyone here.'* An instinct I am willing to bet came from your mother and father. I think you truly *are* destined for more."

Eliza was rigid as a board as she stood facing Kent, the words he said resonated with her so profoundly she knew she could not deny the truth of it. He had echoed her thoughts as clearly as if she were an open book.

"Can you read minds?" she asked, suppressing a shiver.

Kent's eyes sparkled with amusement. He brushed her arm with a gentle hand, "Don't be ridiculous. Only Wizards can do that without you noticing. I'm not even a terribly good warlock, but I am a visionary. I'm just waiting for a discovery that will put me down in the history books. Maybe *you* are that discovery." The hand he had used to brush her arm had stayed still at her elbow, but now he let it go slowly down the sleeve of her arm and, for just a fraction of a second, the bare skin of his fingertips brushed the back of her hand and she saw in her mind a flash of a great castle on a lake. Amusement still lingering in his eyes, he winked at her and left the room.

Before Eliza could call him back to ask what the castle was, a swarm of students started spilling in for the next class. Third year Healing was about to begin. Eliza hurried out against the tide, determined to consult the runes and find out more about her origin and her destiny. Today.

Eliza unlocked the door to her room and she and Pal entered quickly. She closed the door behind her and strode across the room to her single bed. Eliza reached underneath for the wooden trunk where she kept the tools that had been essential to her magic before she arrived at Kentree. She grabbed her runes, some candles, and a handful of crystals. Thanks to Energy Amplification she now had a deeper understanding of what each of the crystals was capable of; they were the first materials they had studied at the beginning of the year.

Eliza spread the runes out in front of her, created a circle of candles which she lit with just a wave of her hand. It was true what Melissa had preached; practice did indeed make perfect. She had practiced this spell so many times she hardly needed to think about it anymore, it was becoming second nature.

Pal laid across her legs where she sat on the floor. Eliza began swirling the downward facing runes in clockwise fashion.

"What happened to my father?"

He searches for you.

"Are either of my parents from North America?"

No.

"Are they both from Europe?"

Yes.

"Did they participate in the war Professor Kent told me about?"

They were unhappy with their situation and desired to change it. They took destiny into their own hands. They lost control of the situation, and the full force of the consequences came down upon them. They should have stopped. They believed they were above all.

Eliza asked Pal what he thought the answer meant. In the end they decided to interpret it as a confirmation. It was the same war.

"Were they from the UK, then?"

Yes.

"Is my father still there now?"

No.

Eliza looked down at Pal and wondered if there was a faster way of determining where her father was without having to ask each country in the world one at a time. Just then, Pal leapt from her legs and ran across the room toward the desk. He pawed at a drawer.

"Isn't there a map in here?"

"Oh! Yes!" Eliza followed the cat and began searching through the loose papers she had thrown into the bottom drawer until she found a yellowed map of the world. It was sadly outdated, labels indicated countries that no longer existed and others that had not yet been divided. Witching folk were so out of touch with the political rumblings of the mundane world that they didn't bother to update their maps. Eliza brought the map back to the spot on the floor she had prepared and found that Pal had already extracted a crystal pendulum from the bowl of crystals. She sat cross-legged again and held the pendulum over the map.

"Where is my father now?" asked Eliza, holding her breath.

The crystal spun around the map a few times before stopping still above Northern Quebec. "He's close," said Pal. "And searching for you... I wonder if he is on his way to Kentree right now."

Eliza threw the map to one side and pulled out a spirit board that she had begun crafting for Energy Amplification and held the crystal pendulum over it. The board had numbers and letters and allowed for more specific answers than the runes. The downside of using the spirit board is that it can easily be influenced by what one wants to hear. Runes are more difficult to interpret, but the pendulum can respond to the users' subliminal desires, instead of the truth. Eliza tried to clear her mind of expectation.

"Why is my father searching for me?"

Nothing happened. Eliza tried a few more times, but the pendulum did not move.

"What was my mother's last name?"

It was no use. The point of the pendulum kept swinging between consonants with no clear pattern and certainly was not spelling any names. She tried a few more times, asking her father's name, too, but each time the pendulum refused to give a clear answer.

"You're too emotional for this," said Pal. "You could ask someone else to do the reading for you."

"What, and risk someone else having control of how my parentage comes to light? You and Kent were right. My mother was probably trying to protect me from the prejudice of being born on the wrong side of a war." Eliza extinguished the candles with a wave of her hand and moved toward her bed, "No, I think if my mother was a murderer and wanted to see herself as a god among mortals then the best thing to do would be to let her rest and write my own story." After putting her tools away, Eliza slumped tiredly down on the bed and squirmed into the covers.

"What about your father? He isn't resting. He's still looking for you. He's not so far away," probed Pal.

"He can't be looking that hard, he's had three decades to find me—with access to magic! He could have found me ages ago," grumbled Eliza.

Pal persisted, "Could he? Until October you had a shield that protected you from discovery."

It was a good point. Eliza refused to answer, though it troubled her.

The cat leapt up and began kneading the blanket next to her, "I thought you found your story too dull. Maybe this is the kind of drama you wanted in your life."

Eliza gave the cat a playful shove, "Shut up! I don't want drama." She looked up at the ceiling and the smile slowly melted from her face as she remembered how meaningless her life had been before coming to Kentree. "Or maybe I do, what would be so bad with a little excitement?"

"You don't sound all that different from your parents," Pal blinked slowly and settled himself down in a bread loaf position. "You want more than an ordinary life, just like they wanted to be more than ordinary. What would satisfy your desires? What do you imagine would be the best version of your life?"

Eliza closed her eyes to imagine what that could look like. She saw herself sitting on a throne in a huge castle, with a dragon, and an army of devoted followers. She was beautiful and powerful, and in the best shape of her life. Everyone recognized her as wisdom itself. She would spend her days creating new, more impressive spells to protect her kingdom and expand its borders. Controlling more and more of the earth. The outdated map that lay on the floor would be changed to reflect her growing empire, her queendom, expanding all over the globe. She would remove all the stupid parking lots and strip malls and return land to ancient, overgrown forests, grasslands and wetlands. People would live in balance with nature, not as its conquerors. Whether by choice or by force.

"In my perfect world," Eliza smiled, "I'm a Disney princess." She stroked Pal's head for a moment and fell asleep, dreaming of a world without industry.

CHAPTER ELEVEN

Dropouts

The days leading up to Christmas were a blur. Eliza had the best time yet at Kentree because finally the last week before the holidays no one was trying to teach any of the students anything new. They practiced spells and enchantments, reviewed information that they had learned earlier in the semester.

To Eliza's great surprise she was now at the same level as most of her classmates. Teenagers, it turned out, were very quick to learn new things but had more trouble remembering what they had covered only two months prior. To Eliza, on the other hand, two months ago felt like just a blink of an eye. She had retained the information admirably. She also noticed Melissa continued to underperform, despite her perfect recall of all the theory and text they had memorized.

"Ignitium!" Melissa cried during the final Sorcery lesson of the semester, but nothing happened.

"You've never had trouble with that one before," remarked Eliza, who was both pleased and a little annoyed that her greatest competitor was no longer in the same league. "Are you feeling alright?"

"Oh yes, I'm just so excited for Christmas, I suppose I can't concentrate," beamed Melissa, though the smile didn't quite reach her eyes.

Despite suspicions that Melissa's powers went the same way as Patty's had, Eliza did not feel it was appropriate to ask outright. It seemed like a very personal subject and Eliza didn't know that she would be able to offer anything in terms of comfort or solution. Thankfully, she didn't have much time to wonder about her young frenemy.

Before she knew it, she was leaving the grounds. Professor Neach threw a ball of energy her way that carried Eliza (who felt once again that she exploded into a million atoms) and Pal back to Brampton. Landing with a swirl, Eliza gathered her bag and Pal, and hurried up the street to her adoptive parents' house.

It was very important, so Kentree insisted, that the magical community remain secret. Eliza had quickly browsed a few pages about Naturopathy, Natural therapy, Aromatherapy, and Permaculture lest her parents ask about what she was learning at college. She felt she had rather missed an opportunity when she chose not to take

Vibrational Resonance, as healing with sound would have been perfectly in keeping with her cover story. That she was studying Naturopathy was a lie close enough to the truth that Eliza felt she was in no danger of saying anything too obviously mystical, and even if she did slip her father would roll his eyes and accuse her of fantasy.

"And you think all this *stuff* will serve you, somehow?" asked her father skeptically as he helped himself to three brussels sprouts from a silver platter, "That people will pay you to do this new-age unproven natural healing?" They sat around the table for a Christmas Eve dinner.

"Well, I just felt like doing something a little different," answered Eliza, pouring herself a generous glass of Cabernet Sauvignon. "At the end of it all I might just end up going back to my old job." A flutter of anxiety flowered in her chest at the idea of returning to work a desk job.

"Don't be so negative," scolded her mother. She kissed Eliza on top of the head before serving big portions of fried potatoes to the family. "I'm sure you'll find your way. Have you made any friends? Any boyfriend we should know about?"

Eliza shoved a forkful of fried potatoes into her mouth and was spared having to answer the question by her younger sister's late arrival to the dinner table. Jesse was the youngest of the family.

The perfect replica of Mr. and Mrs. Paladin. She had her father's nose and mother's dark curly hair.

Mr. Paladin was looking at Eliza with consideration. "I told our neighbour, Henry, about what you were doing. He seemed to think you were onto something. Says he has a niece who does something called Reiki and she's been working for herself a good ten years now. People swear by it, he says. She has a wait list that's months long for new clients... will you be learning Reiki at this school?"

"Yes," Eliza nodded earnestly. "I think next year I'll take some courses on Reiki." She made a mental note to read about Reiki so she could talk with moderate intelligence about the subject this time next year.

Mr. Paladin nodded approvingly, "I'm proud of you. My little girl, an entrepreneur!"

Blushing, Eliza changed the subject by asking Jesse what news she had to share. While her younger sister regaled her with stories of her social life and work frustrations, Eliza let her mind wander. She felt uncomfortable misleading her parents, but more than that she realized she had no plan at all for when she graduated from Kentree.

She had wanted to exist in a world of magic so badly that she hadn't spared a thought to what she would do when she had studied everything she was interested in learning. Maybe she could travel to other witching schools until she became a Wizard. And then what? She ate the rest of her dinner in preoccupied silence.

Christmas day wiped away any fears about the future. Her older brother, Kyle, brought his kids and wife along in the morning to open presents. Pal stayed out of sight of the children. He was still angry about an incident two years prior when he was carted around by the tail. Eliza, not having much to do since she had outgrown receiving Christmas presents, helped herself to a few mimosas and some coffee with cream liquor. She was drunk before lunch was ready. Lunch was a messy affair—her father had also gone a little too hard on the morning booze.

Eliza stumbled to bed at three in the afternoon after belting a few choice Christmas carols with her dad (to the general displeasure of her siblings and nephews). She felt it was the best Christmas day ever. It wasn't until she was throwing up half-digested chocolate a few hours later that she thought perhaps she had missed the meaning of Christmas after all.

The rest of the holidays with her family was a happy affair, and when she returned to school two weeks later, Eliza was refreshed, eager, and a few pounds heavier.

Things continued to look up for Eliza as the

return from the holidays had somehow erased the memories of the teenage student body. The faculty were prepared for this, and the first week back was another week of revision. Wand movements, fireballs, wood sculpting, crystal identification, herbal remedies; all back to basics and refreshing what the young brains had lost. Eliza was feeling so confident about her abilities finally having caught up to her classmates that it was the third day into the new semester before she noticed that something was off.

"How many people have dropped out from your year, Eliza?" asked Faye at breakfast.

"—What? Dropped out?" asked Eliza, who stopped in the middle of buttering her toast. "Why? Do students often drop out after the first semester?"

Faye and Mashu exchanged a significant glance. "Not at all. Usually people stay three years and drop out in the fourth year when the coursework gets considerably more advanced." Faye explained patiently, "I was telling Mashu yesterday that I noticed at least four people in my year haven't come back this semester."

"And today I paid a little more attention and I noticed at least five people in my year haven't come back," grumbled Mashu, brow furrowed in concern. "Patty is one of them."

This worried Eliza, who had completely forgotten about the plight of Patty and Melissa Sweet. Would a loss of magic not explain the increased dropout rate? Was there an epidemic of students losing their magical abilities? She left Faye and Mashu in the Grand Room, since they had no classes until the afternoon, and went to her Cooperation with Beings Magical and Mundane class.

Eliza paid closer attention to attendance in her class. There certainly seemed to be more empty seats than the previous semester. Unfortunately, Eliza had been so focused on coursework before Christmas that she didn't have a full recollection of who might be missing. She regretted being so self-centered and resolved to pay more attention to others from now on.

"Have you noticed if some people haven't come back this semester?" Eliza whispered to Melissa when they were supposed to be learning to ask a frog to croak.

"Yes," said Melissa in a distant voice. "Three that I know of—one was a good friend."

"Did they say why they weren't coming back?"

"No," Melissa said grimly. "I can only imagine why they preferred to stay home."

Eliza was far from convinced by Melissa's response. For one thing, the tone clearly indicated a touch of sarcasm. Melissa was still not back to her usual smiley and bubbly self. Though Eliza found that she preferred this more toned-down version of Melissa, it made Eliza uneasy; something foul was at play.

Reaching a decision, Eliza resolved to uncover the truth of the matter. If someone had been robbing people of their magical abilities, she needed to make it her mission to find them and stop them. It wasn't right, she thought, and she could never live with herself if she allowed her powers to be taken again.

Eliza observed Melissa closely over the next couple of days. Melissa was still smiling and preaching optimistic quotes ("Don't stop until you're proud!"), but the smiles never reached her eyes and her words sounded hollow. She hadn't successfully produced magic since the week before Christmas break but was careful to hide it from other students (she even insisted when Eliza probed that nothing was the matter).

Melissa continued to excel in theory and was remarkably improved in physical magicks. She was still able to combine metals and crystals and woods to form wands, staffs, and amulets that radiated the power of their ingredients. She could harvest and use many magical plants. She even had no trouble communicating wordlessly to a wild coyote in Cooperation with Beings; convincing the animal to roll onto its back and accept a good belly rub.

In Sorcery, however, Melissa was abysmal. Professor Kent's expression betrayed his repulsion of Melissa's inability to perform magic. Eliza could not help but smirk at the sight; she had been regularly offended by Professor Kent's behaviour toward herself. As an outsider, she saw that when Kent belittled students it was his flaw, not theirs. He desired power and sought to distance himself as much as possible from weakness. Eliza glanced sideways at Melissa and felt a shock when she saw that the girl was resolutely trying to hold back tears; her mouth in a downward grimace and eyes blinking upward.

When Eliza and Melissa returned to Sorcery the following week, Professor Kent looked further unnerved by Melissa's continued presence in his classroom. He paled at the sight of her walking back into the room and his gaze was magnetized to return to her every few seconds in the lesson. He hovered over their desks as they worked on a tricky new spell that was meant to pull apart an object into its component pieces. Eliza had succeeded in peeling an onion with the spell and was now trying to separate the pieces of a toy car. Melissa, however, was still staring resolutely at the small yellow onion that had been given to her nearly thirty minutes earlier.

"*Adividis*" she said, in a calm, measured voice. She twirled her wand and jabbed it toward the onion just as they had been taught.

"Flawless execution," said Professor Kent, nostrils flaring. "Can you tell us why it didn't work?"

Eliza watched curiously as Melissa smiled widely up at the professor. "I must not be clear with my intention. I'm sure I'll get it eventually."

Kent's expression was nauseating. He swept back up to the front of the class and sat behind his desk, allowing Melissa and Eliza to continue working.

"M—Melissa. I, um, is there somewhere wrong with your magic? It's just—the last time I remember you actually casting a spell was before Christmas," whispered Eliza.

Melissa shrugged, feigning nonchalance. "I think a few people have been losing their ability to do magic over the last couple months. I know Principal Crinwere must be very concerned about causing panic if it is being kept a secret. Lots of people haven't come back this semester because of it."

Melissa was speaking in a robotic, unfeeling tone. She hesitated a moment before she continued, "It's only happening at our school, from what Principal Crinwere told me. No adult witches or warlocks have reported this happening, and nothing in the news about it happening anywhere else..." A shiver ran down Eliza's spine when Melissa added in a hollow voice, "although if everyone is keeping it secret, it could be a while before anyone realizes how far it goes."

Silence hung between them.

"Is Principal Crinwere doing anything to help you

get your magic back? It's not… *permanently* gone… is it?"

"Well, if I can lose my magic overnight, I'm sure it can just as easily come back. I'm not going to sit around going to a Mundunce high school and lose a year of magical education like everyone who decided to drop out. *When* my magic comes back, I will be as good a student as I ever was. *Adividis!*" Melissa declared, confidently poking the onion. The onion remained unmoved.

"How many people know…about your problem?" asked Eliza.

"I've been trying to keep it to myself. My friends are in different classes, so they haven't noticed. I think it would freak them out," grimaced Melissa. "I told Principal Crinwere last semester when it happened. I was told that the whole faculty would look into it immediately. I think it is more worrying now that nearly twenty students in all have gone home. No one knows what is causing it. No one knows if it's still happening. No one knows if it's stopped."

Eliza creased her brow, "It could still be spreading?"

"It didn't happen all at once. It was sporadic." Melissa whispered, careful that Chad who was seated at the desk immediately in front of them could not overhear. "One by one at first, a few days apart. The day I lost my magic, three other people lost theirs. I don't know if anyone new has been targeted since Christmas, so maybe whatever twisted experiment someone was doing is over."

Melissa's gaze drifted away, her mind somewhere far away. Shaking her head, she blinked and looked back at Eliza. "It doesn't matter. They'll find out what happened and reverse it. Everything will be great!" Melissa beamed forcedly.

It was a smile Eliza could not return, concerned as she was about her own magic. She had everything to lose from this mystery remaining unsolved, the perpetrator might still be collecting more victims. "This happened the day you lost your grandmother's necklace?"

"Yes—" said Melissa, her eyes widening. "How—?"

"Someone else I know lost something before Christmas too, and she didn't come back," Eliza twirled her wand distractedly in her hand and the toy car she was meant to be practicing on took off and flew into the back of Chad's head before landing on the floor with a clatter. Melissa snorted loudly and Eliza quickly looked the other way as Chad whipped around in his seat to glare at them. After an awkward moment and an apologetic smile from Eliza, Chad finally returned to his own work. The girls resumed their whispered conversation. "Is it possible that objects that we cherish could somehow... I don't know... *imbibe* our magic? So when you lose it, you lose the magic too?"

Melissa shook her head. "I don't think so, but it might be related. Maybe it's like voodoo, where a doll represents a person. Maybe the objects represented *us* and…" she threw up her hands. "I don't know. I can't imagine how someone could do this. Or *why*."

"Well," Eliza lowered her voice, afraid Professor Kent could overhear despite presently being occupied in coaching another student. "Apparently in *some* countries, people have a prejudice against some people having magic. They think it should only run in families."

"No one in my family is magical," said Melissa. "Not until me."

The girls exchanged a significant look. When they packed up their things at the end of the lesson, Melissa grabbed Eliza's arm to hold her back when they were out in the hall.

"I'm going to talk to Principal Crinwere again. They would be able to find out how many of the other students were from non-magical families. And if they all lost objects before losing their powers… if either of those things connect us… well… it could be the first step to reversing the curse!" Melissa beamed brightly at the thought. She turned, ran down the hall, and her blonde hair disappeared into the crowd in a brilliant display of optimism.

"Eliza," said a man's voice behind her. It was Professor Kent. "Could I have a word?"

Eliza followed him back into the empty classroom, holding her chin high. She was sure he would scold her for spending most of the lesson distracting her classmates by talking.

"I think I found your mother's identity," said Professor Kent. Eliza's heart jumped painfully in her chest. "I sent for old newspapers a few weeks ago." He opened the top drawer of his desk to reveal several yellowed newspapers. They were accompanied by a small book titled *Dark Sorcerers of The Century.*

"You're not telling me she's in a friggin' book about evil people," exclaimed Eliza.

"Eliza, you're looking at it the wrong way." She felt her stomach flip at Professor Kent's informal use of her first name. "When you work in a garden and your shovel kills an earthworm—are you really causing harm? The earthworm would say yes, you are evil. But your vision is much greater. You are digging to remove sod and plant a tree. You know that beneath the shade of the tree, there will be far more life in the earth. More humidity, more diversity of insects and animals, and a more comfortable climate. Had you let the earthworm live and simply maintained the lawn into perpetuity, you would have been doing evil in a subtle way. Maintaining the status quo when it is at the expense of measurable improvement is its own kind of villainy."

"My mother killed *people*," she said. "Not earthworms."

"Your mother was powerful and had a vision of a better future. A few people were sacrificed so many more could thrive."

"She *murdered children*."

"I know it is hard to understand—"

"No, what I don't understand is how you can seriously be *defending* these atrocities. If there was a war today, would you be willing to kill people just because they were born into powers that their parents didn't have?" Eliza demanded.

"Not at all, I do not think they should be killed." Kent reached out a hand and grasped Eliza's arm firmly. "They simply should not be allowed to join in our ancient traditions and practices; millennia of knowledge passed down and perfected through generations is handed over to newcomers whose ancestors contributed nothing to our people."

"But how can you condemn someone with the power to make rain, to make plants grow, to *fly!* How could you condemn them to a life of complete boredom in a rat race?" pleaded Eliza. "To belong in a society that teaches them their only value is selling their time. That all they contribute is nothing more than earning and spending money.

That they exist apart from that fantastic force that turns the earth and breathes life. I *knew* there had to be more. How could you wish a deprived life for anyone?"

"Eliza, you knew you were destined for more because you *were* destined for more." Kent gave her arm a little shake, "I went to a school for magic all my youth, and now I've been teaching here for five years. I have seen with my own eyes. Children who come from Mundunce families arrive here with shock and awe on their faces. They are delighted by the minimal display of magic. They never *imagined* a world like this could exist. By not teaching them, they would lose nothing. They did not fight against established society; they did not earn their place here as you did." He continued to hold Eliza's arm, his thumb stroking her bicep gently.

"I saw you the first day you arrived," Kent's eyes bore into hers. "That cat of yours has a connection to you that is undeniably mystical. You walked in here like you belonged. You felt *owed* inclusion. You knew you belonged to more than an ordinary life and you cultivated your powers to the point where you broke free of the enchantments your mother conjured to hide you! This *despite* your mother's best efforts to make your mind irresponsive to magic. To make you unaware of your own marvelous abilities. She did her level best to prevent you from finding our people, but it was so written in your genes that you found us anyway. You are nothing like children from Mundunce families. You must not compare yourself with them."

Rooted to the spot, Eliza did nothing to contradict Professor Kent.

"You speak of not condemning people to a rat race, but most people are willing participants," Kent murmured gently. "They choose every day to be a part of it. They lack the vision and imagination to choose a different life! Why gift them something they have no capacity to appreciate?"

Eliza's fingers grazed the stack of newspapers that held answers about her mother's mysterious past. Professor Kent's arguments were surprisingly convincing and she found herself being swayed. She could not agree with his views, but she knew it was better to keep him on her good side. He was proving to be a good source of knowledge, and he was much more pleasant when he wasn't belittling and insulting her. But the knowledge that these papers could show her mother in a negative light repulsed her. Eliza dreamed of being a hero, not the child of a murderer. She was torn between wanting to devour all the information available about her parents, and wanting to conjure a ball of fire to consume the book and newspapers until they were reduced to ash.

Professor Kent snatched her hand away from the

newspapers when the edge of the topmost page began to curl and smoke.

Startled out of thought by the sudden movement, Eliza looked into Professor Kent's eyes once more. He was looking at her with a determined expression, her hand still in his. He was so close she could now appreciate that in a certain light his brown eyes had a golden halo around the iris. The expression with which he was looking at Eliza captivated her. She was frozen there. Locked in his eyes, the window of the soul. She felt a tingling sensation where his hand held hers, and the sensation turned into a pleasant shiver that travelled down her spine. She felt something else, too. It was somehow connected to a slight shimmer that began to appear between them, like a haze was radiating from her body and moving toward his. She felt warm. She felt safe. She wanted him to know everything about her.

Eliza snatched her hand out of his, comprehension dawning suddenly.

"You said you couldn't read minds!" she accused.

Professor Kent chuckled, brushing his hair off his face, "I said I wasn't very good at it. I have to make physical contact *and* maintain eye contact. How did you detect it, though?"

Flustered, Eliza shook herself, "A side-effect of having magic hidden from me my whole life. After going into the enchanted pool I've been able to *see* magic. Did you know a lot of this old cathedral is being held up by enchantments? Honestly, I find it hard to sleep sometimes, imagining that it could all come crumbling down." She was babbling, she knew. Her cheeks burned from the embarrassment of nearly having her mind read.

She was distracted when Professor Kent looked surprised by the information. "Is that so?" He looked around at the walls and ceilings, Eliza presumed he was trying to see the enchantments she spoke of. "Can you show me? You hear of Wizards being able to detect ancient curses but I'm not aware of anyone actually *teaching* students how to do it. Seeing through illusions... This might be exactly the sort of breakthrough my career needs."

Bewildered by the sudden change of subject, Eliza agreed, "Yeah, I can show you." She paused, looking at the stack of newspapers Professor Kent had brought her. "Just let me put these in my room first."

She held up her hand to the papers and concentrated with all her might on the bed in her room. Eliza willed the newspapers and book to teleport there. When Eliza opened her eyes, they were gone. She smiled, satisfied. She had learned to do that only the week before and was pleased to have pulled it off perfectly.

She and Professor Kent left the room, heading up

the hallway toward the staircase that led down to the ground floor. Eliza led the way, pointing out defects as they went. "That doorway has a huge step crack going up to the ceiling but there is a fuzzy energy holding the brickwork together to stop it breaking further apart." They reached the bottom landing, Eliza crossed to the other side of the hall.

"This is the wall that has a concealed doorway leading into the principal's office—you can touch it and feel a warm buzzing in your hand—," she continued up the hall and stopped before reaching the double doors to the Grand Room, "—this window is actually a solid wall—if you look just to the side of the window, from your peripheral you can see the brick beneath the fake outside view, and *that*—" said Eliza coming to a stop at the entrance into the Grand Room. "—is what I am most concerned about. The ceiling is literally caving in. The only thing holding this entire section of the roof up—," she pulled out her wand and traced a coloured line in the air and sent it up to the ceiling to outline the area she was referring to, "—is magic. See how it's all hazy and hard to focus on?"

Eliza felt Professor Kent standing very close to her. She had given him her back during the walkthrough and he had stopped within an inch of her. He was leaning close to see the traced shape on the ceiling. She felt his breath move her hair and tickle her neck, giving her goosebumps.

"Anyway," declared Eliza loudly. "That should give you enough to start studying your new branch of magic. I'm going to go read that stuff you gave me…bye." And she turned and walked quickly away. Why was her heart fluttering stupidly in her chest? Faye's words about her and Professor Kent looking like a couple echoed absurdly in her mind and gave her a nervous whooping sensation in her chest. She was working very hard to suppress a smile. Finally, she couldn't help herself and broke into a big stupid grin.

It wasn't until she was in her room that she realized she never stopped to wonder why Kent tried to read her mind. She saw that the pile of newspapers and the book she had sent there had missed her bed by a meter and were scattered on the floor; evidence that she had yet to perfect the teleportation spell. Now faced with the daunting task of reading about her mother, Eliza realized she was unable to gather the courage. She picked her way around the papers and sat down at her desk, to write an essay about cooperating with songbirds.

CHAPTER TWELVE

Vigilante Justice

The pile of newspapers on the floor of Eliza's bedroom remained undisturbed for several weeks. She got up, went to class, studied, slept, tidied, and all while maintaining the little patch on the floor untouched. Pal had taken to swatting the newspapers, scattering them into a larger and larger circle in the hopes of pressuring Eliza into reading them, or else that perhaps some headline would catch her eye. Eliza resolutely refused to look and by the third week had to cast a hovering charm on herself to drift slowly across the room a few inches above the scattered papers.

"This is getting out of hand, you have to read them," Pal scolded her.

"I don't see why I should," said Eliza stubbornly. "My mother so desperately did *not* want me to find out I was related to a pair of murderers that she turned me into a Mundunce to keep it from me. If her dying wish was that I never know her, then I will honour that wish."

"And when Professor Kent asks why you haven't read any of this?" pressed Pal. "He went out of his way to find her for you."

"I did not ask him to do that, and Professor Kent has not been very interested in my heritage lately, thank-you-very-much," Eliza replied with snark. The truth was, she was a little hurt about it. It had been nice to feel that her origin might be important, or special. Worth noticing. But there had been no further interactions outside of class.

Not only was it a non-starter with Professor Kent, but she was also tired of banging her head at the dead end that was the mystery of the missing powers. Eliza had wasted no time in involving her friends in the conversation she had with Melissa Sweet.

"Melissa and I might have found a link between people who have stopped coming to classes." Eliza had announced importantly to her friends that same day, causing Faye to look up in interest. "We think it has something to do with their missing objects, and possibly even have something to do with their heritage."

Faye pursed her lips waspishly and asked, "Why does Melissa keep going to classes if she's lost her power?"

"She said she doesn't want to be behind when she

eventually gets them back," answered Eliza.

Nodding, Faye asked, "What does it feel like, did she say?"

This question surprised Eliza, who kicked herself. Why hadn't she thought to ask? "I'll find out next time I see her."

"Let me know what she hears from Principal Crinwere. And how it feels to be without magic. It would be interesting to know if you can live a normal life without—" Faye cut herself off. "Just let me know, will you?"

Eliza watched Faye rise gently from the seat and leave the Grand Room. She had a feeling of foreboding seeing her friend gliding away. She knew Faye was determined to find a way to stay firmly in one world without constantly flickering between them. Could she go looking for trouble in her quest to find personal peace?

Eliza was now one of the best students in her year and in the month since students returned from Christmas break no one else had lost their magic. Whatever had caused several students to drop out was still cause for murmurs, but since it wasn't spreading, people quickly forgot the incidents.

Melissa Sweet was still optimistic, though Principal Crinwere had refused to divulge much information about the other students who had dropped out.

"Even though you said that we're trying to help solve the case?" asked Eliza, indignant.

"I think they're just trying to hide the fact that Kentree has discovered very little so far," Melissa shrugged. "But when I mentioned our suspicions about it being people from non-magical families, I got an eye-roll as a response. Principal Crinwere asked why anyone would target us specifically. Then, when I said I thought the loss of magic was connected to the loss of an important object I didn't get a reaction. Like maybe they already knew that? I think there's a good chance the missing objects are a link between victims."

"And you think the principal is actually working on it?" asked Eliza, doubtfully.

"Oh yes," Melissa nodded earnestly. "It would be bad press if Kentree lets this kind of thing go unchallenged at the school."

This irritated Eliza. "What bad press when this is a secret school? And if the people who it happened to come from non-magical families, how would they be able to put pressure on Kentree to stop the crime? Their families were never told what kind of school their kid was *actually* going to."

Melissa's brow creased. "Do you really think there is no incentive to help the victims?"

With a shrug of her shoulders, Eliza pressed. "Not really. This is just a job to the staff. It doesn't affect the faculty one way or the other if there are a dozen fewer students one year..." Eliza swelled with the opportunity to display her proficiency outside of the classroom. "No, if you want to get to the bottom of it what we need is some vigilante justice."

With wide eyes and a frightened giggle Melissa looked around nervously, "What, like, take matters into our own hands?"

"That's right." Eliza leaned in conspiratorially. "You have nothing to lose. They've already taken what they wanted from you."

"You have something to lose though, they could take your magic too."

"Maybe," admitted Eliza. "But what they've done to you is wrong and someone has to do something about it."

Proud to appear brave and courageous, like a hero in a tale, another thought crept uninvited into Eliza's mind. The possibility of glory if she restored a few dozen students' powers warmed her chest. They would admire her, celebrate her victory; they would forever be in her debt.

Eliza imagined herself being praised as someone who doesn't just talk about making a difference— she is someone who takes action and makes things happen! Smiling at the thought, she saw herself surrounded by everyone in the school clapping and calling out her name. Professor Kent would place his hand firmly on her shoulder and say, "I *knew* you were destined for greatness."

But there her fantasy hit a snag. Professor Kent. Because if her working theory was that the students targeted were from non-magical families, then the obvious suspect was Kent himself…

"Eliza!"

"What, sorry?"

"I was just saying, I know your faery friend has been trying to get information from Principal Crinwere about this too. Has she told you anything? It's just—I overheard the principal telling her it was none of her business to ask what happened to the students who've dropped out. The principal said—" Melissa paused. She looked guiltily at Eliza.

"You don't think it was wrong of me to eavesdrop, do you?" asked Melissa.

"Not at all! That's what vigilante justice is all about!" cried Eliza.

Reassured, Melissa continued, "The principal said that considering Faye had applied to study removing magic *last* year that she would do better not to get involved… I was thinking… maybe your friend has some insight on *how* this magic could even have been performed?"

Eliza shook her head, "No, Faye's trying to find a way to control the faery magic she inherited." Eliza spent a few minutes explaining how Faye was in constant flux between two worlds; her magic was as unstable as her physical presence. "Removing magic was just one of many theories she has wanted to study to try to get a grip on her faery half. It's like a curse. She's never looked at how to take *other* people's power away. It's for herself. She would rather be a Mundunce, I think, than live the rest of her life in two worlds."

"Hm…" Melissa looked disappointed, "She might have studied enough on the subject that she would know the type of magic involved. Can I talk to her about it? Maybe I can sit with you guys at supper tonight."

"Sure," said Eliza, imagining how odd it would be to have this pretty fifteen-year-old sitting with her and her friends, "I don't see why not."

The talk over supper that night did not yield much in the quest for justice. First Faye told Melissa about some accounts she had read where contagious parasites had taken the magic of some witching folk. Had she been permitted to study the subject, it would have been Faye's first point of call to find and interview all the known victims and find the parasite responsible. Melissa indulged Faye in a long interview. Faye took notes in a leather journal as she asked one question after another: When was the moment she realized anything was wrong? Was it immediate, or gradual? What did it feel like? Were there any other symptoms or side effects, besides the loss of magic?

What Eliza could not foresee was that Melissa Sweet would become a regular member of their group. Sharing supper that evening provided Melissa with an open invitation to sit with them for every meal, and she did just that. It was useful for the group, as Faye and Eliza were both very keen on the subject of the magic thief, but it was a few days before Melissa admitted at breakfast the true motive for her repeated appearance. Her friends had finally discovered she had lost her magic and were treating her as a pariah.

"My boyfriend broke up with me in front of everyone when he found out," she said miserably. "I guess he thought it was unattractive," she stabbed at a piece of sausage on her plate.

Faye and Melissa were spending a lot of time together going through all the books in the altar library of the Grand Room. Neither was particularly interested in studying for their exams or finishing their homework. It had quickly become an obsession that bonded the two and they spent every evening searching for any clues to what kind of magic could cause what had happened. The girls worked an entire evening writing a list of all the students who hadn't returned. They wracked their brains trying to remember their names so they could try to get in touch with them. The next day they sent letters to each in turn and were presently waiting for them to reply. There was talk that if they hadn't heard back from anyone by summer break, they would take a trip across the country to locate as many as they could. The solution, Melissa and Faye believed, was out there. All they needed was one good witness.

Eliza felt stabs of jealousy as she sat at their usual table in the Grand Room studying for her classes with Mashu. She was interested in solving the mystery too, of course. But she didn't want to sacrifice her own success in order to do it. Mashu was resolutely uninterested in the subject and muttered that it had nothing to do with his kind, and their politics in such cases were to stay well away from danger and controversy. Eliza wanted to ask what 'kind' Mashu belonged to, but she remembered how Mashu evaded the question last time and held her tongue.

With rising frustration, Eliza could no longer stand agonizing over the why and how of the magic theft. She was far more interested in finding out the *who.* Her prime suspect remained Professor Kent, though there was no evidence to point that all the victims were from Mundunce families. Eliza had taken to trying to catch him in the middle of some terrible act, coming upon him unawares when he wasn't in his office apartment. He did seem more jumpy than he had previously been and was behaving nervous any time she approached him.

"Miss Paladin, to what do I owe the pleasure tonight?" he asked tensely when she discovered him in the library altar. She had been approaching stealthily to see what he was studying. He hastily stuffed the papers he had been working on into his leather messenger bag.

"I finally read what you gave me," said Eliza. It was true. She decided it was the best way to open a conversation with Kent. Each time they had talked about her ancestry, he had dropped his guard about his own life. She thought maybe this time she could exploit this interest to get him to admit his involvement in the school's mystery.

There was no question that the woman Professor Kent had uncovered had to be Eliza's mother. Eliza felt goosebumps when she saw the images of a woman who looked almost identical to herself staring back at her from the front page of an old newspaper. Pale, thin-lipped, and wide-eyed like Eliza. Though there were several articles about how she came to be a prominent revolutionary, and how she came to be captured, one article in particular haunted Eliza.

Five Found Dead as Criminal Escapes

Tragedy befalls our community as Leonarda Gibbon, 42, was witnessed fleeing the country late Thursday night. The witch in question, a strong supporter of power segregation, has become one of the most notorious escapees since the war ended. All efforts to catch the witch have resulted in injuries to those who attempted the feat.

"I didn't even have a chance to set my staff on her," said Olfrus Craine, who has been in hospital for the last month. "All I had time to do was clap my eyes on her and then I woke up here!"

Gibbon has been on the run with her husband since the war ended almost two years ago. Though unaccompanied by her spouse, it was noted Thursday night that Leonarda Gibbon appeared to be with child. Efforts to stop her escape onto a waiting ship were hampered when two children became involved.

"I don't know how it could be possible," reported Tollin Took, friend of the Dearborn family, "The children belonged to Mr. Dearborn, who was in charge of bringing the vile woman in! She must have stolen them from their beds, certain he would not attack her if his children were in danger."

When Dearborn and his team came upon Gibbon at the docks, there was some negotiation for the safe return of the Dearborn children. According to a confidential source, Gibbon offered to return the children only once the ship was well out to sea. Dearborn would have nothing of it. Tempers ran high. It is unclear who fired the first curses, but by the time smoke settled it was too late. Leonarda Gibbon was out to sea propelling the ship with unnatural speed toward the west, leaving behind five dead bodies. Dearborn and his two children were among the deceased.

While it cannot be confirmed that the curses that killed the children came from Gibbon herself, the burden of culpability for all five deaths have been placed upon the criminal. As such, the witch is now wanted for a total of nine murders in addition to previous crimes. Mr. Gibbon was never witnessed at the scene. Anyone with information regarding the whereabouts of Leonarda Gibbon should contact the authorities immediately.

Eliza felt shaken by the article, written twenty-nine years prior. Her eyes lingered on one sentence in particular. *Leonarda Gibbon appeared to be with child.* Unbidden, a smile played on Eliza's lips. It was inappropriate, to be sure, but she felt a strange little thrill to see she herself appear in a newspaper article even before she was born. Shaking her head, she suppressed that little spark of joy by reminding herself that the contents of the article were so grim in nature that she ought to be ashamed.

"What was that?" Professor Kent asked, distracted, "You read the homework assignment?"

"The—no, the information about my mother!"

"Oh, yes, sorry I had rather forgotten." His brow creased. "I gave that to you weeks ago. Have you only just read it now?"

Eliza blushed, "It might surprise you to know it isn't easy to come to terms with your mother being a war criminal after spending a lifetime dreaming of being a hero."

"Your mother believed herself to be a hero too," said Professor Kent.

Eliza pondered this for a moment. Here was her opening. "She would have been better to do what the person here is doing."

Kent's eyes flashed, "And what is that?"

"Well," said Eliza calmly, "it would have been kinder to remove someone's power without killing them. You were right, magic isn't a blessing to everyone and much less if the punishment for having it is death."

Professor Kent's body relaxed, "I am glad you are beginning to see my side."

With a casual air Eliza said, "It's actually my friend Faye who convinced me. She wanted to study how to remove magic, but Principal Crinwere said it was a prohibited subject."

"She wanted to study removing magic?" he looked interested. "To what purpose?"

"She can't control her magic," answered Eliza authoritatively. "You haven't had her in your classes so I suppose you wouldn't have seen it. She's trapped between our world and the fae world. Well, not trapped. She exists simultaneously in both and neither. She describes it like flickering rapidly between both worlds. She's tried everything, but nothing works. Her last hope to live a normal life is to have her magic removed completely," Eliza concluded.

"She willingly wants to sacrifice that part of herself," cried Professor Kent. "It's not the same as what your mother wanted, though it would be a new way of justifying the removal of power."

"It's just a moral argument at this point," said Eliza. "Similar to a conundrum like: should you save someone's life if they have to live in pain for the rest of their lives? Or this one: is an animal better off safe in a cage or free where it could die from predation or famine?" Eliza was satisfied to see Kent listening with interest. "I knew I was destined for something more than a Mundunce life, meanwhile, like you said, the kids who grow up believing they are Mundunces until they come to this school would be unchanged and unaffected if their magic were just to…" she waved her hand in the air conjuring a cloud of smoke, "…disappear before they get accepted to Kentree," and she made the smoke clear.

Professor Kent smiled approvingly, "I'm glad to see you coming around to my way of thinking." He ran a hand through his thick brown hair and leaned back against the banister separating the altar from the Grand Room. "Sometimes I worry the idea of keeping magic for select individuals is too radical for most people. There are genuinely those who think that *more* people having access to magic would not diminish the power of those who already have it. But how can one be more powerful than another if we are all given equal gifts?"

Eliza nodded in agreement, but her lips were pursed tightly against a reply.

Sliding his hand across the table to touch hers, Professor Kent smiled warmly at Eliza. "Your mother would be so proud. You could take on the good fight. Keep magic exclusive. Not something that any wicca-wannabe can dabble in at their local *Magick Shoppe*." The emphasis on the last two words indicated distaste. He stroked the back of Eliza's hand and a strong revulsion overcame her, but she fought not to snatch back her hand. She had begun cultivating her own magic in such shops and using witchcraft books probably written by Mundunces whose magical ability was likely near zero.

"How would it work?" asked Eliza, "The world you envision? Would you raise the level of magic needed to be accepted into a magical institute, or would people have to manifest by a certain age?"

Professor Kent reached his second hand forward and clasped Eliza's hand firmly between his. They were hot and slightly moist, but Eliza maintained contact. It was important that she win his confidence. If he was in any way involved in the school thefts of magic, she would find out.

"While that is a lovely idea, I think it is not efficient

enough. Better to eliminate magical ability from all those who come from non-magical families as a blanket policy. Those who know their destiny lies in the magical community are more likely to kick up a fuss at rejection than those who never knew of any such legacy."

"So even if a young witch from a Mundunce family registers magic twice as powerful as the warlock from a magical family," said Eliza, trying to compose her face into an expression of polite curiosity, "she would be denied what her genetics imparted on her so that the warlock would never have to feel inferior to a newcomer in our society?"

"Precisely," agreed Kent. "What have her ancestors contributed to our world to make her worthy of inclusion?"

Eliza's stomach rolled, but she pressed on nonetheless. "Would everyone born into a witching family automatically be allowed to keep their magic? Or would there be circumstances where you might take their power too?"

Professor Kent released her hand at last, and pulled out a British newspaper from his bag, "Here, for example, is a classmate with whom I went to school." Kent indicated a wedding announcement that included a picture of a couple radiating happiness. "He is marrying a Mundunce woman who has no idea he is a warlock. They will live in a Mundunce village. Does he need his magic, now?"

"Didn't you say this is exactly how your family made its fortune?" probed Eliza, "Excelling at Mundunce things by using magic?"

Professor Kent looked annoyed at this retort. "We never sullied our blood by mixing it with Mundunces!" he declared, drawing some stares from students sitting at nearby tables. He lowered his voice and leaned closer to Eliza, "We do not *compare* with the likes of this flagrant disregard for our proud past and heritage."

"Right, I understand. Your classmate and his future kids get cut out. No magic for them, even if they are born with it."

A nod was Professor Kent's only reply.

Eliza drew herself up in front of Professor Kent, her eyes almost level with his, "Yes, I see it now," she held her chin high. "Power only belongs to people who are worthy of it. No one else should have the privilege of knowing what we can do, they don't *deserve* what our parents worked hard to build just because they *exist*." Now came the moment of truth. Eliza needed Kent to confess. "I *wish* I knew who had been taking away student's magic. At first, I wanted to find them so they could help Faye with her problem but, can I be honest with you?" Professor Kent nodded again, observing her quietly.

"I was *sick* of how obnoxious Melissa Sweet was in our classes at the beginning of the semester.

Always out-performing me. Not because she is special, or intelligent, or anything. Her only advantage was one month longer at this school. *I* deserved to be here learning to use my power and because of a society that demonized my parents' segregationist vision *I* ended up being the one removed from *my own people!* And that daughter of Mundunces thought she was *better* than me. Taunting me with '*Things can only get better!*' I want to meet whoever took her magic and shake their hand," said Eliza with conviction. "It's been such a relief not having that gnat badgering me every lesson, showing off. Mocking me."

Eliza hated herself for saying these things, but in trying to convince Professor Kent of her changed opinion she had expressed some repressed thoughts of her own. She pushed them back down now. Jealousy and pettiness were hardly the traits she wanted to define her.

Professor Kent watched her in pensive silence. Several long seconds passed before he spoke.

"I would like to meet them too, to know how they did it," he said. "It could be an invaluable tool in the new world order I want to—I mean—*we* want to build."

Eliza's heart sank. "You have no idea who it could be?"

Shaking his head, he said, "No, and I find it incredibly frustrating that they discovered how to do something in the very same school where my studies have led me nowhere!"

"Don't you have more information than students do? We've only figured out what's happened because Melissa Sweet refused to drop out. Is there anything connecting the people who have lost their ability? Like, they aren't all Mundunce-born are they?"

"They are not," he said, "some are from non-magical families, some are mixed, and some are full blooded. There doesn't seem to be much linking the victims other than lost objects."

Eliza nodded, nothing new from that information. She bade him a good evening and was about to leave when she remembered to ask why he had been trying to read her mind the last time they spoke. Kent had a glint in his eye when he answered bewilderingly.

"I was looking to see if you could be aligned with my view of the world. Forgive me, but I see your ambition is much grander than mine."

Eliza returned to her room, disappointed. What a waste of time. She had learned nothing. There was something else bothering her, too. She had tainted her own rosy view of a fair and equal world. After declaring that power should remain with the powerful, her whole body felt like it was crawling with insects. She sat at her desk and rubbed her temples with her fists. Pal bounced up immediately to her side.

"Don't you worry, Eliza," he said. "Even though it was a dead-end, we'll find a new lead. I'll put the word out among the animals around the school. I'll make an alliance with the pigeons if I have to (the filthy creatures). Someone must have seen something suspicious. We'll find the bad guy."

Eliza smiled and scratched Pal behind the ears. He always knew what to say to cheer her up.

CHAPTER THIRTEEN

Mashu's Missing Piece

The next day Eliza arrived at breakfast after Melissa and Faye, who were serving themselves pancakes with maple syrup. Eliza told them quickly that she had suspected Professor Kent and after speaking to him last night she had come to the conclusion that he knew no more than they did. All she succeeded in doing was getting confirmation that the victims were not connected in any way other than the missing objects. Faye looked entirely unsurprised by this, and Melissa had the good grace to thank Eliza for her effort. Eliza was just pouring syrup over her own pancakes when Mashu came jogging in with sobering news.

"Someone spiked my tea last night," he said, gruffly. His huge hands were shaking and his eyes were darting around nervously. His white hair stuck up in a mess, like he hadn't bothered to comb his head that morning.

"What?!" cried the girls at once.

"I went to the herbalism room to mix myself a tea for stronger focus. I wanted to spend the night studying for a test I have tomorrow. But the last thing I remember is drinking one gulp of the concoction and then nothing. I woke up in my bed with no memory of how I got there." He remained standing, too agitated to join them at the round table.

Eliza paled. "Is anything of yours missing?" she asked.

The expression that crossed Mashu's face told all. The girls gasped.

"What?" asked Melissa, "What did they take?"

Mashu held out a furry hand. The fur was white as snow, the skin black as coal, and each finger ended in a dark brown claw. Each finger except the index finger, whose claw had been cut clean off close enough to the finger to cut a vein.

"Can you still do magic?" asked Melissa.

He removed his wand from the holster at his belt with a wooly hand and did a complicated little movement toward a coffee cup. The coffee shot skyward and arched back down elegantly, a little coffee fountain.

"Whoever took your... um... nail, hasn't had a chance to complete the curse yet," breathed

Melissa.

Eliza closed her eyes and allowed her mind to reach out to Pal who was still sleeping in a ray of filtered sunlight in their room. He stirred when he felt her probing him. *Someone drugged Mashu and took a claw from his hand. They haven't performed the curse yet. We need to find them. Now.* She felt the cat send her a message of understanding and she knew he would shortly be dashing from their room to spread the word among the animals of the school. It was essential they find one eyewitness who could indicate the culprit in time to prevent the curse being performed.

"We'll find them before they can perform the ritual. Please, sit down," said Eliza to Mashu, who continued to rock on the balls of his feet. As an afterthought, she added, "I wonder why you are being targeted?"

Melissa gasped and struck herself on the forehead, "Oh—listen! There's nothing connecting the victims. Eliza, that's what Professor Kent told you. Principal Crinwere basically said the same thing to me; all different backgrounds, different ages, different levels of magical power, different genders."

Melissa took a deep breath, her voice trembling slightly. "What if the one thing uniting all the victims is that no two are alike?" She tried an apologetic look to Mashu. "You're...something else. It's like whoever is doing this is testing the magic on as wide a pool of witches and warlocks as they can. They're experimenting."

Melissa's expression became temporarily puzzled. "Although...If that's the case, why wasn't your group the first targeted? The general sentiment is that the three of you... Not my words, *don't belong here.* Mixed breeds and an old—I mean... old*er* student. A lot of people don't think you three should study alongside them. And if I wanted to test a new theory of magic, you three are very much representative of a diverse group. And no one would miss you if you left."

A shiver ran up Eliza's spine at this uncharacteristically dark assessment by Melissa. She'd always been too honest for Eliza's taste, but this was missing Melissa's usual positive spin. A hint of something dark stirred in Melissa's usually bright blue eyes.

Eliza locked eyes with Faye, wondering which of them would be next on the criminal's list. Faye hadn't yet said a word, and Eliza saw that she was stiff as an oak. She appeared to be grappling with an emotion stronger than she could bear. Eliza exclaimed as Faye's gentle, almost imperceptible, flickering stuttered and the girl disappeared entirely from view for a full two seconds.

Eyes wide, Faye took deep breaths to steady herself. The flickering continued to sputter without rhythm or pattern until, slowly, she returned to her usual immaterial, constant presence. Mashu patted Faye's shoulder reassuringly, his own hand still trembling.

"We're going to stop them. Today," declared Eliza, and she meant it. It was one thing when mere acquaintances were being affected, but Mashu was one of her only friends at Kentree. It was no longer a question of playing at being the hero. This time, it was personal.

None of them went to any of their classes that day. Eliza and Mashu, who were better equipped for spellcasting, spent the morning trying every tracing spell they could find in order to locate the lost claw. Faye said she would go out to the forest and communicate with as many magical creatures as she could find. She would ask them if they had seen anything unusual. But first, Faye said with shaking voice, she had to go check on something in her room. She glided out of the hall with unnatural speed. Melissa, who was unable to perform magic and had exhausted the resources available for research, merely disappeared without a word to any of them. Presumably, she was searching manually.

Faye returned at lunchtime shaking her head, which was decorated lightly with snow. Eliza and Mashu had not uncovered anything, either. Melissa merely shrugged when she arrived in the hall and joined them as they discussed options for a new strategy. Mashu was still able to perform magic, so they knew they still had a chance of catching the culprit red-handed. They had just decided to enlist Principal Crinwere's help when Pal appeared from under the table. He bounded up onto an empty chair, and gently deposited a little mouse on to the table next to Eliza's hot chocolate. The mouse was unharmed apart from being wet with Pal's saliva.

"He has something to tell you," said Pal. Eliza looked down at the little mouse. He was squeaking slightly, indicating Mashu, holding his little paws up and doing a weird little dance. Then, the mouse mimed drinking from a cup and fainted dramatically onto the table. Eliza reached out to the mouse but in a flash he was back on his feet and stooping into a deep bow.

Everyone at the table stared at the little mouse in bewilderment. The mouse looked at Eliza expectantly, looking very pleased with itself.

"I—I only know how to speak with you," she told Pal. "I don't speak mouse."

Her cat fixed her with a condescending expression, "Why don't you *try* to listen instead of letting your mind tell you that you can't?" His tail flicked in irritation.

Pal gave the mouse a slight nod and the mouse began his story again. Eliza let her mind enter a middle state of awareness and meditation. She was trying to recreate the state of mind she had been in when, while weeding in her garden on hands and knees, she heard Pal speak to her for the first time. A state of mind she had sometimes heard referred to as 'flow'. There she began to hear the mouse's words.

"A strange figure cloaked in heavy fabric approached the Yeti boy and emptied a small bottle of potion into his cup while he was waiting for it to cool. The boy was so focused on his book he did not notice, and the figure retreated to the shadows. The boy drank from that cup and—!" the mouse swooned one more. He picked himself up, dashed in an excited little circle, Pal watching with body tense and pupils wide, and the mouse stopped to look expectantly at Eliza again.

"The figure was cloaked, you couldn't tell anything about them?"

A bang startled Eliza and the mouse. Searching for the cause, Eliza noticed Melissa double over in pain. "Ouch," Melissa said, clutching her knee. "Sorry, a nervous twitch. I had no idea you could speak to animals," exclaimed Melissa.

Eliza turned her attention back to the mouse as he began to speak again. "Yes, they were smaller than an adult human. And they smelled of cream of leek soup," the mouse licked his lips and whiskers, apparently remembering the delicious smell. Eliza nodded, everyone had been served cream of leek soup the night before for supper.

"Did you see what they looked like?" asked Eliza. "Was it a boy, or a girl?" Mashu, Melissa, and Faye leaned forward in anticipation.

"I did not see what they looked like, I was eating a piece of ginger biscuit someone had dropped on the floor, and the figure was cloaked."

Eliza deflated, disappointed, "And did you see them take anything from Mashu? Or where they went after?"

"No, once the boy fainted—" the little mouse mimed fainting again, "the figure drew out a large staff. I stopped eating my biscuit to admire it. It was a fine thing, carved with five interlocking pieces of wood. I smelled oak, yew, elm, maple, and elder. They were fused together by metals, weaving around them and crystals—so many crystals I could not count them for you. For nearly every inch of this exquisite staff was adorned with their magic. The staff struck the floor thrice, and the Yeti boy began to float. Well—," the mouse corrected itself. "He didn't quite float, he was dragged along the floor with an invisible force the staff-bearer controlled. They left, and I returned to my biscuit."

Eliza thanked the little mouse. He stuffed his cheeks full of Eliza's leftover ham sandwich and, surprising everyone at the table, the mouse permitted Pal to pick him back up by the scruff of the neck and carry him away the same way he had arrived.

Faye looked shocked at the display, "You weren't kidding about your cat being willing to make any alliance to get information! What did the mouse say?"

Eliza repeated the mouse's story to everyone, trying to remember every detail. Mashu looked increasingly uncomfortable. He barely touched his food and kept casting little spells every few seconds to check that he was still able to. Faye watched him with heartbreaking pity. She gently touched his shoulder. "Nothing's going to happen to you," she promised. "If they were going to take your magic, they would have done it by now."

"How do you figure?" asked Mashu, more aggressively than was necessary. "How could we possibly know that? Some spells only work by moonlight. It might be a potion that takes months to brew. Most of the kids who lost their powers lost them over Christmas break, maybe it's something to do with the solstice and they're collecting from people for a June blitz. You've found nothing in your weeks of research, so we can't possibly know that I'm not going to lose my powers. I'll have to go live in the forest as an under-grown yeti runt who left his people to bring back knowledge and instead returned without a drop of magic."

"I—oh, I don't know," said Faye miserably. "But I

really feel like you have nothing to worry about! Call it intuition. I think they didn't complete the spell, and more importantly they won't. It's only worked on humans as far as we know!" Mashu shook his head and stood up from his seat. He left the Grand Room without a word, but Eliza suspected he was holding back tears. Faye cast a glance between Melissa and Eliza, and addressed them both in a lowered voice, "Mashu is a cross between yeti and bigfoot." Her voice was a barely audible whisper. "There was a breeding program to improve the genetic diversity of the two species. The resulting offspring were unpredictable. Well, you've seen Mashu. They are extraordinary and as diverse from one another as they are from witching folk. A regular hex or curse that could hurt a human might have a very different effect on him."

"But that's a good thing. We could still stop them," said Eliza bracingly.

Melissa tutted uncharacteristically, "You're talking like once it's gone, it's gone forever. Where was this urgency a week ago? Twenty students have dropped out and lost their magic! Have we not been working under the impression that the magic can be recovered? You're all gung-ho about stopping Mashu from losing his powers. What if he lost them? What if he had come to us this morning and had no powers? Would you give it up as a bad job and leave him to live a new life without magic? Are you guys gonna just abandon us to mundane life while you all get to live your fairytale fantasies? Oh, but if one of you two—" she indicated Eliza and Faye, "—gets threatened, then I suppose you'll take this whole thing seriously again."

Melissa pushed herself up from the table, scraping her chair loudly against the floor. "Forget you and your group of misfits," she spat. "I'll fix it myself." With that, Melissa tore out of the hall, several heads turned to watch her go.

"If she still had magic, her hair would be crackling right now," commented Eliza, concerned that Melissa was losing her mind along with her magic.

The rest of their day did not prove much more fruitful, and by ten o'clock that night Eliza collapsed exhausted onto her bed. She had been so full of arrogant optimism that if they could just put their heads together and give it their all for a day, they could truly crack the case. But they had learned nothing new, nothing of value, and still had no leads. Just another object to search for, a big fancy staff no one other than the dramatic little mouse had ever seen. Pal leapt lightly onto the bed at her side and pawed her arm reassuringly.

"Someone might yet see something," he said. "We might still catch them. And now we know they're probably a student, if they're smaller than an adult."

Eliza stroked Pal's head appreciatively, but she closed her eyes knowing that the following morning would be no different.

Melissa was not in her usual seat the following morning when Eliza entered the Herbalism classroom. She was nowhere to be seen all day, in fact. Mashu, thankfully, could still perform magic. Faye was still visibly shaken from the event and struggled to control her flickering; from time to time, she sputtered out of view and returned with a sob.

Eliza saw Melissa slipping in and out of the Grand Room over the following week. She only came in to take food and left the dining hall just as quickly, carrying her meal away in a napkin. She had completely cut herself off from the rest of the students and had stopped attending all her classes. She was often seen wandering the corridors or devouring books in the library. Her hair became messier by the day and her appearance progressively more disheveled.

For their part, the trio did not stop trying to get to the bottom of the mystery. Weeks passed and no spell, no divination, no communications to the great beyond yielded any decipherable answers. Eliza even tried a guided séance but all she could glean from this was the rush of wings circling her, confusing her, bamboozling her. The answers to her questions were confusing, like the runes didn't believe Mashu's incident was connected to the others. It wasn't until one night in early April when Eliza lay in bed mulling over the possibilities that she had a stroke of inspiration.

She sat up so quickly that Pal, who had been laying on her chest, was launched to the foot of the bed. Eliza wrenched off the covers and threw herself in the direction of her divination tools. Quickly, with shaking hands, she lit the candles and arranged the crystals and runes before her. She asked the runes for confirmation of her theory. Pal joined her, ears bent backwards. She was right. The answers had been confusing until now because she hadn't been asking the right questions.

Eliza launched herself out of her room, tearing up the stairwell to the third floor of the dorm building. She half-jogged until she reached Faye's room. Pal did not follow, he was too annoyed.

Eliza knew her friend, who had been a pile of nerves since Mashu had been drugged, would be grateful to know what she had just discovered. The person who drugged and took Mashu's claw was not entirely unrelated to the curse that affected the other students—but neither was it the same perpetrator.

Melissa Sweet, dear optimistic Melissa Sweet, desperate for more people to pay attention to her plight, had tried to motivate Mashu and Eliza to join in the daily obsession of solving the mystery by making it more personal.

Melissa drugged Mashu. She had crafted herself a staff that combined every amplification object she could get her hands on. She had not lost every ounce of magic, and the staff amplified what little was left, allowing Melissa to create a potion and move Mashu to his room in the dead of night. Eliza slid to a stop in front of Faye's door and knocked. There was no answer. Hesitating only a fraction of a second, Eliza tried the door and found it unlocked.

Inside was a room of identical proportions to her own, but Faye had a clear glass dormer window instead of stained glass. Eliza presumed the window must overlook the river, but since it was dark out, all Eliza could see when she turned on the old electric light was her own reflection. There was a marked difference in the contents of the room. Eliza's room was full of books, notes, and drawings from her first year of classes. Faye, who was now in her third year, had fully occupied every inch of space and added many shelves where Eliza had only blank walls. Jars of specimens, limbs, hair, and body parts floated in salted solutions upon Faye's bookshelf. A pair of floating eyes followed Eliza's movements, giving her goosebumps. The desk was covered in thick leather-bound tomes that were so ancient they were loose from their spines. Eliza had never seen these in the school's library and presumed Faye must have acquired them somewhere else.

There were also letters on the desk. Unable to quiet her curiosity, Eliza flicked through a few of them. It looked like the students who had dropped out had replied to the letters Faye and Melissa had written. They described their symptoms and their ongoing feelings of emptiness since losing their magic. It was odd, Eliza did not remember either Faye or Melissa mentioning they had received any replies. Drawing close to a large book, which lay open on a page describing how to mix a complicated potion, Eliza's eye was caught by a small movement to her left.

There, in the corner of the room, was a small altar. Eliza had seen altars in many a would-be witch's living room; she had one in her house in Windham. She knew now that those Mundunces with altars probably instinctually felt the magic in the objects they displayed there. Though not powerful enough to allow them to manifest fully, perhaps potential witches and warlocks would eventually receive an invitation to study at Kentree if they practiced enough. To see an altar in a practicing witch's room was a new sight for Eliza. She had never occasioned to enter any of her classmates' rooms before and never supposed that the altar tradition would be present in magical families, too.

But this altar was peculiar. It had crystals, pendants, wands, and the usual witching knickknacks. But it also had tufts of different coloured hair tied together in a bow, a few personalized coffee mugs, and bits of old jewelry. As Eliza drew closer, a wave of warning washed over her body. The fine hair on her arms and on the back of her neck rose. Her breath appeared in a fog before her, the air bit coldly at her skin. The chill that surrounded the altar was most ominous, but Eliza rationalized it away as part of her imagination.

There was a small hand-held vanity mirror propped up in the middle of the shelf above a handwritten leather journal. It was this that had caught her eye from across the room; shapes were moving within the mirror. She was repulsed by the sight of it, just as a small voice whispered to her that it held many powerful secrets. Instinct prohibited her from reaching out to grasp it; she cast a floating charm on the mirror to raise it and bring it close enough to examine the shapes within the reflective glass. The mirror floated closer, and she suppressed a cry of horror at what she saw.

Figures, more figures than Eliza could count, were screaming in the mirror. She saw them sobbing, tortured, mad, ragged. Clawing to be released from within. Eliza didn't know how to make sense of this horrifying little mirror—nor, indeed, why it should be displayed in a place of honour on her friend's altar. She was just coming to the conclusion to put it back down and ask Faye about it later when one of the figures pushed itself forward through the crowd and the white, petrified face of a pretty blonde came into clear view. Eliza could not help but yelp in horror—the cheeks were hollowed out but it was unmistakably the face of Melissa Sweet screaming silently from within the mirror, tears streaming from her wild eyes.

The figure was pulling at her hair in agony. Eliza, still using the charm on the mirror, pushed it back toward the altar where it fell onto the shelf with a heavy clunk. Breathing heavily, skin clammy with sweat despite the unnatural cold surrounding the altar, Eliza froze in panic. What could she do? What could be done? Should she take the mirror and run? It was the smoking gun, clearly framing Faye as having performed a most evil kind of magic. What were these people doing in the mirror? That Melissa should appear there, surely, must connect Faye to the disappearance of Melissa's power?

Eliza's eyes flickered down to the notebook that lay in front of the mirror. The writing was miniscule, and many notes were scratched out and replaced with others even more cramped between the lines. One word halfway down the left page jumped out at her; it was underlined three times in triumph. It read:

SOULS

CHAPTER FOURTEEN

Stolen Souls

Crossing the room again, Eliza grabbed the books on Faye's desk and turned them over to read the titles. *Krafting Dark Artes* and *Fearless Invention— Magickal Exploration Beyond Limits of Civility.*

Faye was not to be deterred by Principal Crinwere's refusal to let her study dangerous magicks. She had found source material to teach her how to create what did not already exist—a way of controlling her volatile faery-witch magic. But the lengths Faye had gone to, to steal people's *souls.* Eliza could take no more supposition. She needed to leave, to clear her head, to think rationally. Could it be that Eliza was so inclined to believe the good in Faye that she never paused to consider Faye would be willing to go to any lengths to solve her problem?

No, not any lengths. A small voice reminded her. *Melissa said as much, "I'm surprised your group wasn't the first targeted. If I wanted to test a new theory of magic, you three are very much representative of a diverse group."* Faye did not cross the line of trying the magic on her own friends. Mashu, being a mixed breed like herself, would have made an excellent test subject.

With sudden haste, Eliza turned toward the door to leave. Horror gripped her stomach. Some powerful instinct told her that leaving from that door was not an option; that she would surely be discovered by Faye who must be returning from late night studies at any moment. As tumultuous as Eliza's thoughts were, she knew herself to be unable to hide the discovery she had made. With a huge leap of faith in a magic she had not yet grasped full control, Eliza closed her eyes tightly and concentrated very hard on the courtyard outside of the cathedrals. She thought she could hear the faint hum of Faye's invisible wings approaching the door to the room.

Eliza had never teleported. She didn't even know the theory. It wouldn't be covered until third year. Some extraordinary self-preservation instinct took her over and she felt her body explode into a trillion tiny atoms, and just as quickly they reformed. She took a ragged, gasping breath and found herself breathing the chilly spring air. Eliza opened her eyes and sobbed freely in gratitude to see she was outside the school.

Collapsed on the flagstone courtyard, Eliza wept for several minutes before collecting herself. Pal had found her now, and his gentle mewing awoke her to the urgency of the moment. Without a word to Pal about what happened, she directed her footsteps to the school. She knew what she must do.

Her first visit would be to Professor Kent's office. She knew she should probably go straight to Principal Crinwere, but she hadn't spoken to the principal since her first day at school. Eliza didn't feel at ease heading there to accuse Faye without an ally. She knocked twice at his door.

Quietly, Eliza stood listening for signs of life, but heard nothing from within for a long minute. Starting to wonder whether she ought to go alert Principal Crinwere first after all, she finally heard the shuffle of footsteps. The door opened a crack.

"Oh, it's you." Professor Kent rubbed the stubble on his cheek. He was dressed in warm cotton pyjamas, "I'm not on the clock, this can wait until tomorrow." He started to close the door in her face.

"*Please*, I just found out who the person stealing magic is!" sobbed Eliza.

"You found them? You're *sure?!*" Kent opened the door wider.

"*Yes,* I'm sure!" Eliza pushed roughly passed him to enter the office.

There were several books and a diary that lay open upon the desk. There was an open door leading to what looked like a bedroom. Presumably, Kent had been preparing himself for sleep when Eliza knocked. She turned to face him; he was closing the office door behind her.

"The worst part is I found out totally by accident. It was Faye! All along! She didn't even have to *try* to hide from us, we've been sitting with her every day this year and never once did we suspect our friend could be the one behind this! God, it's so obvious now," declared Eliza, berating herself. "She never pretended her intention was anything other than curing herself and she *insinuated* repeatedly that she would be willing to go to any lengths to do it!"

"And the worst part is that you found out by accident? I advise you not to repeat those sentiments to anyone," said Professor Kent putting things into context. "People have been robbed of their identities. The way you discovered the culprit is the least of their worries. They'll just be glad to have justice."

"Fine! So, what do we do?"

"It's best we are cautious in our next steps," deliberated Kent. "We do not know how dangerous she is. She could be tremendously powerful by now if she's not just succeeded in removing power, but absorbing it…"

"I saw shadows of the victims in a mirror," said Eliza, "It looks like those people are trapped in there. I saw Melissa Sweet inside the glass."

"Hm…" Professor Kent paused, a hand on his chin and a look of annoyance crossed his face. "What a crude way to store them. So unsecure. Were there any protection spells on the mirror?"

Eliza thought back, trying to imagine the mirror as it hovered in front of her. She couldn't remember seeing any of the telltale signs of spell work.

"No," she said finally. "There were no spells on it that I could see but I felt a powerful warning against touching it. Maybe she's able to create magic that wouldn't leave traces?"

"It is possible… It would explain how she evaded detection all this time with so many looking for her. I wonder… do you know her age?"

"No," answered Eliza. "I've assumed she was in her early twenties. She's definitely a little older than most of the students here."

"Yes, but fae are famous for their youthful faces. She could be in her eighties for all we know. Their lifespan is three times ours. She could be advanced at sorcery, able to cover her traces. She might have had the chance to study magic at several institutions around the world before coming here."

Eliza was conflicted and confused. She had considered Faye a good friend, an ally against the regular overachieving teens. But she could not resent Faye for never divulging her age— Eliza had certainly never asked. She thought Faye's face looked around twenty, but as her friend was translucent and difficult to focus on in her fading, immaterial way, it was not impossible that Faye could be much older. Eliza regretted not asking Faye more about herself and her life before Kentree.

Professor Kent paced around his office and asked Eliza many questions. He asked Eliza to describe Faye's room and all the contents she remembered seeing there. Had she been there before? Was anything prominently out of place? Did she remember the colour of the eyes that floated in the jar? What was on the altar, besides the mirror? Eliza described what she had seen as best as she could but felt frustrated that she could not more accurately remember the room. She felt like an idiot, she hadn't entered her friend's room with the intention of a sleuth and had glanced at everything quite casually before spotting the mirror. Then, once she had ascertained that her friend was a total psychopath bent on stealing people's souls, she had only the instinct to run, not to probe deeper.

"Professor, *please*, stop asking me questions! *I can't remember, I don't know!*" begged Eliza, "I do not have a photographic memory! I'm not Harriet the Spy! I went in there to tell her about Melissa Sweet setting up that Mashu would lose his magic if we didn't solve the case immediately." Eliza let out a frustrated roar. "I am the *worst* person in the world to be investigating something like this!" she declared. "And come to think of it—Melissa probably suspected it was one of the three of us who was the attacker. She was probably trying to see our reactions in response to one of us being targeted. It should have been easy to tell from our reactions which one of us it was."

Eliza remembered how Faye had reassured Mashu in no uncertain terms that he would not lose his abilities. Had it really been so obvious all along?

Kent looked at her with an expression of deep disappointment, "Maybe you lack... certain basic... observation skills but dumb luck has allowed even the most un-extraordinary people to become immortalized in their accomplishment. There is still hope for your legacy."

"Thanks," spat Eliza, feeling the hairs on her back standing on end as they would on an angry cat. Only Kent could find time to be an ass in a moment like this.

"We must report this to Principal Crinwere," said Professor Kent, "and from there we can form a plan that will allow us to fully assess the situation. We must not be unprepared when meeting our enemy —to do so would be to invite doom and failure."

Eliza spread her fingers and performed jazz hands in the air in front of her, "So dramatic! Let's get going, then, why waste time?"

Eliza and Pal turned together and marched out of

the room, chins held high, toward the principal's office. They did not wait for Professor Kent to gather himself or to catch up when they rapidly made their way down two flights of stairs. Stopping abruptly in front of the blank wall where the door to the principal's office was hidden, Eliza said in a loud clear voice, "Excuse me, Principal Crinwere, I need your help with something."

The shuffle of steps behind her marked Professor Kent's arrival as he caught up to her. Eliza's heart leapt in her chest at the sound of a gentle rustling coming from the other extremity of the hall. She turned toward the noise and saw Faye appearing from around the corner, her eyes black as night and skin pale as glowing moonlight. Eliza turned her head the other way to see Professor Kent in a disheveled state, putting a robe over his pyjamas and carting two large books.

Slowly the stones in the wall in front of her slid open to form an archway, the other side of which stood the principal. Faye and Professor Kent reached Eliza at the same time. Professor Kent calmly kept his composure at the unexpected appearance of the very subject in question.

A pregnant pause was broken when Principal Crinwere asked, "To what do I owe this late pleasure?"

Eliza thought hard, her heart pounding in her throat. How could she ask for an audience with the principal without alerting her friend that she knew her to be the one responsible for the attacks? Or perhaps Faye already knew that Eliza had been in her room and had rushed down the hall to stop her telling anyone, in which case it was very lucky Eliza had not been caught alone. Eliza felt the warmth of Pal's tail brush against her ankle and took a deep breath.

"I need to speak with you Principal Crinwere, urgently," said Eliza.

Principal Crinwere's eyes betrayed a trace of surprise for only a moment before they moved over to Professor Kent, "Mark, am I to understand you were also coming to see me?"

"Yes!" he exclaimed breathlessly, "Quite urgently."

The principal looked at him piercingly and seemed to assess that whatever he had come to discuss was very serious indeed. Eliza felt a pang of annoyance. Finally Principal Crinwere addressed Faye last, "And you, dear, is this a mere coincidence or were you also heading this way?"

A smile played around Faye's youthful mouth, "I was also coming to speak with you."

Each of their faces were examined with a calculating expression. Eliza tried to speak through her eyes that she *must* be allowed in. But when Principal Crinwere turned to invite a guest into the office, it was not Eliza.

"Mark, I sense the business you bring me is of a truly urgent matter, I know you rarely elect to conduct business during your hours of leisure," said the principal amicably. "Do come in. Miss Paladin, Miss Griggs; please come back tomorrow during regular hours. I hope you understand that sometimes there are subjects more pressing than timetable conflicts and rejected study applications."

Professor Kent walked into the room, shooting a look of caution in Eliza's direction. The archway sealed itself behind them. The door became a solid stone wall once more and Eliza found herself alone with Faye. Mortified, Eliza spent a few long seconds staring at the stone wall. She did not want to have to look into Faye's face, but survival meant she must. Even if only for a moment, Eliza would have to pretend she was still on her friend's side.

"Well, that's too bad," cried Eliza, and with a huge effort she shrugged in what she hoped was a nonchalant way. "I guess we'll have to come back tomorrow."

Her friend's eyes scanned her face, which Eliza hoped was now composed into a calm mask. "I took Empathology for four semesters." Faye stated with an edge in her voice. "I know you're seriously panicking right now. What's going on?"

A jolt of nervous energy flashed up Eliza's chest as she tried to conceal her surprise. She had to work to either calm herself or come up with a good story. Would any of it even matter if Faye already knew that Eliza had stumbled upon the truth?

"I just—I think… I have reason to believe my magic will be taken next," lied Eliza, but she thought the shaking in her voice made the lie sound convincing.

Faye's eyes widened in genuine shock, "What? Why?"

Eliza cast around for a story. She remembered how it felt when Kent had taken her wand for a week and was inspired. "I—I can't find my wand. You know, the first one I was given when I started at Kentree. Well, obviously I have others now, too, that I made in Energy Amplification but my first one… well, I have a special connection to it."

Her story was met with eyes narrowing in suspicion, "I mean, what if—what if that's what they needed to take my powers away?" Eliza's tone rose in panic at the end of her question. She had no control over the shaking in her voice. It was this touch, however, that seemed to convince Faye of the authenticity of Eliza's distress.

"Look," Faye reassured her kindly, "tomorrow we can investigate like we did when Mashu's claw was cut off. It seemed to scare them off that time, we can do it again."

"Yes," breathed Eliza, trying to look reassured though her entire body was trembling with fear.

"You're right… we could still stop it." Faye smiled warmly at her and touched Eliza's shoulder impossibly gently. Eliza forced herself to look into Faye's dark eyes and smile back at her. "Why were you going to see Principal Crinwere?"

"Oh, the usual," said Faye easily. "I keep trying to get approval for new branches of study that would allow me access to more archives. But the principal keeps accusing me of trying to dabble with *dangerous, forbidden, or world-ending magic*" Faye rolled her eyes as she imitated the principal's husky voice. "I was just bringing a new proposal," and Eliza saw that it was true—Faye had a large envelope enchanted to float along behind her labelled MULTI-WORLD DOORWAYS – PROPOSAL.

"That's a new one," said Eliza. "How many have you tried now?"

"Oh, I've tried all kinds of proposals now. Research into removing one's innate magical ability was a hard no, the principal didn't even open my essay. Multiversal travel, the genetics of interspecies mutations, anything I thought could help me exist in one world only."

"Knowing why you want to study these subjects hasn't softened Principal Crinwere on agreeing to help?" asked Eliza.

"Apparently if applied to any situation that is not specifically mine, any magic that could be discovered or invented as a result of my research could pose a threat to our entire universe, or our entire society," Faye shrugged dismissively, "but I think it could also increase our potential hugely. The other world I flicker to is barren. Hardly any plants, no rain, and aside from some insects there is not much life there. But imagine being able to use this power at will. We could gather resources from other worlds. Send people to other places in the universe. It could be fantastic."

Eliza frowned, "And what's the risk?"

"If where I am going is another universe in a multiverse, apparently two universes could collapse into each other causing the destruction of both. If it's another planet within the same universe, then I could fold the fabric of reality over itself and—well, total destruction sums up most of Principal Crinwere's arguments against my studies."

Eliza nodded and said quite reasonably, "It does seem like a large risk if the only reward is a few people getting to travel to new places."

Faye's eyes flashed angrily, "Obviously! But it's all just an argument to find me a cure, isn't it! If I can stop flickering, I can stop doing this whole bloody thing. No one has to live the way I live, you see me here and you think I'm fine and dandy. My pain is invisible, constant, and without a cure. No one is particularly motivated to find one because they know this—this *curse* could never happen to them."

"Please don't take this the wrong way, but what if your proposals were approved?" insisted Eliza. "What if you experimented with these obscure magicks and it hurt people? Or sent them somewhere they couldn't come back from? What if in the end you managed to find the key to controlling your flickering and you end up stuck in that barren planet instead of this one, unable to come back?"

Eliza could have melted under the look Faye gave her. It was revulsion mixed with superiority. "You know nothing," said Faye. "Do not try to meet me in this conversation, I have spent longer than you can imagine trying to comprehend the problem that affects me. You have spent mere *minutes* pondering the problem. Goodnight."

Eliza watched Faye float immaterially away until she disappeared into a tunnel leading to a staircase to her dorm room. Something prickled at Eliza's conscience. This was not the first time she had heard such a thing. It was the same as when Patty snapped at her, or when Melissa stormed out on their group.

Eliza did not understand how all of them could have the same anger toward her when she was only trying to help, to show empathy. Clearly, it was never Eliza's intention to pretend she knew more about other people's problems than they knew themselves. Perhaps it was like her own annoyance toward Melissa's use of motivational quotes. Nobody who feels frustrated and ignored wants empty platitudes.

After a few moments reflecting on her guilt, Eliza turned on her heel and returned to Principal Crinwere's office. This time she spoke very quietly to the blank wall, "Can I come in? It's Eliza and I'm alone."

The doorway revealed itself again; smaller and less grand than before, just large enough for her and Pal to squeeze through. Once in the warm embrace of the office, the doorway sealed itself tightly behind them. Eliza looked around the room. Principal Crinwere and Professor Kent were seated at the armchairs by the fire, a coffee table littered with literature about souls between them. Neither looked up at her entrance. Both sat on the edges of their seats devouring any information they could lay their eyes on.

"Can I help with anything?" asked Eliza, awkwardly standing by the armchairs.

"Your friend is hellbent on realizing her personal ambition," said Principal Crinwere without looking up from a heavy book. "She wants to cure her condition and has shown that she will stop at nothing to achieve it. She regards other people's suffering as a necessary evil in her quest for a selfish resolution. Do you have any information that could help us stop her? Do you know any of her weaknesses?"

Eliza stuffed her hands into her pockets. "Um, no, not really."

"Mark kindly informed me of your conversation with him earlier tonight," continued Principal Crinwere. "We did not know who was behind the mysterious loss of magic. Faye had never been shy about stating her purpose here. Even so, it was never suspected she had gone so far with her experimentation. All while balancing a full course load! Now that we know what she has done, we must approach her carefully. She might be more powerful than any of us know. And no one, including herself, truly understands the magic she is trying to create."

The words *total destruction* echoed in Eliza's head. "Faye's not trying to *absorb* anyone's power. She won't be stronger than you. I saw those students. Their souls are still in her room. Trapped in a mirror."

Professor Kent spoke, "Unfortunately Eliza, we cannot know for certain. We do not understand the mechanics of *how* she was able, using simple objects that belonged to the victims, to remove those students' magical abilities. We cannot be certain of what else she is able to do. She has harvested their souls, certainly, and encased them in the mirror. Whether the magic remains with the soul or can be extricated is unknown. Principal Crinwere has reason to believe Faye has been dabbling in more than one prohibited branch of magic and the combination of several of these could prove disastrous to those of us who are too noble to pursue them."

"This is forgetting to mention that the mere fact that Faye is willing to test this sort of magic on innocent victims makes her volatile and dangerous," added the principal.

"Okay, so what's the plan?" asked Eliza.

At this, Principal Crinwere closed a book and looked up at Eliza for the first time. "The plan is to learn what we can from the resources we have available at our disposal tonight. Then, when Miss Griggs is in class tomorrow, we will enter her dorm room and confiscate everything we find there. When that is done, we will keep Miss Griggs in her class until she is alone there with her professor. We have potions to make her compliant. We will ask her to assist us to undo the curses she has created and from there we will reassess the situation based on the discoveries we make. Your part in this plan is simple. Do not alert her that there is any plan in motion," the principal held up a hand to prevent Eliza from interrupting. "Act as you usually would. You will be informed when the threat has passed. Hopefully the students who lost their magic will be able to return to the school at the start of the next semester."

There was a pause.

"Is there anything further you wish to know before retiring to your room?" inquired Principal Crinwere.

Wishing she had something clever to contribute, all Eliza could say was, "It sounds like a good way to stop her without causing a scene… I just wish I could help, somehow."

Professor Kent snorted in derision, "Unfortunately there is very little an untrained witch can contribute to such a situation. In alerting us to your discoveries you did just about the only useful thing you could do. Though you dream of being a great hero in a grand battle, the truth is you have played your part and played it well. Now you must do the responsible thing and let people greater, more talented, and more experienced than yourself take the lead."

Eliza stood frozen to the spot. Professor Kent was an insufferable man. At times, she felt a friendship kindling, then he would reveal himself to be nothing more than a bully. For the first time, Eliza had the presence of mind not to take his insults personally.

She had seen how he could treat her with kindness one day, and condescension the next. His treatment of Melissa Sweet when she lost her magic also betrayed a flaw in his character. It was absurd to presume he could hate her. There had been nothing in any of their interactions that would cause such powerfully negative emotions. Eliza suspected this outright rudeness was a mask for something else, that he was trying to throw her off by causing turbulence to her emotions.

Eliza searched Professor Kent's face curiously, and noticed Principal Crinwere doing the same.

"Thank you for explaining the depth of my insignificance," said Eliza. "I won't disgust you with my presence any longer." She gave him a mocking bow and turned to leave the room. She saw the wall waving there out of focus as the magic that hid the doorway swirled before her. She knew this magic must look invisible to most, but she stepped into the swirl, allowed it to hug her, and took a second step. She and Pal were back in the cold hallway.

Eliza looked down at the black cat by her ankles, "What do you think, time for some sleuthing?"

"He is up to something," answered Pal. They climbed the stairs back up toward Professor Kent's office.

"I don't get it, one moment he's interested in me, holding my hand, finding information about my parents and the next it's like when I first started and he thinks I'm filthy."

"Maybe he's not attracted to untrained witches who have discovered something that he wasn't able to," suggested Pal.

"Ha-ha," said Eliza humourlessly. They reached Kent's office and Eliza placed her hand on the doorknob. She felt her way into the metal and guided the mechanism inside. The bolt unlocked. She opened it and they stepped inside. Eliza conjured a cold ball of smokeless fire to float in the room and illuminate the space.

"What are we looking for, exactly?" asked the cat.

"I don't know, but he's acting fishy. Just look for anything odd," said Eliza.

Pal leapt around the bookshelves, reading book titles, while Eliza opened the drawers of Professor Kent's desk. She found stacks of student essays that he was clearly in the middle of grading, and handwritten class outlines showing the curriculum for each of the four levels Professor Kent taught. Eliza opened a drawer on the other side of the desk and saw a collection of black journals. She remembered seeing a journal open when she intruded upon him earlier. She grabbed the topmost one and found it to be incomplete. He had only written in three-quarters of the pages. Eliza's fingers leafed roughly through the journal to the last entry, which had been written two days prior. She read the entry aloud for Pal's benefit.

After probing all the staff at this institution I am horrorstruck to accept that I am being outdone by a student. If a pupil at this school has unlocked a way to remove magic, and proven that it can indeed be done, they have excelled beyond my decade-long studies. An entire career dedicating myself to precisely this subject has been a failure. By some trick of fate I am to be a witness in the success of another.

Their methods and motives continue to evade. I see no connection between their victims. Some have had great power. Others have intelligence, others are hardly worth noticing in any respect. If only I could discover this genius. They must be stopped, of course. But once they are caught, their research, their book of shadows, would be there, within my grasp. It will take a certain glamour off the whole thing, not discovering the means of producing this great curse myself, but it is what you do with what you are given that truly matters. This student squanders a great discovery and plays small.

"Well, that's totally chilling and useless," Eliza said, throwing the diary back into the drawer unceremoniously.

Pal hopped onto the highest bookshelf and found himself battling cobwebs, "Yes," he said, "we've always known Professor Kent to want segregation, there's little there to surprise us. Except, you might have noticed that you gave the one person who is least to be trusted with the information of who is the culprit with precisely the information he has been looking for."

"Shit, you're right!" exclaimed Eliza, stupidly. "Oh, this is bad! Faye's been messing around with magic to try to fix her own problem (and hurt others along the way), Professor Kent wants to use the same magic to create his messed-up world view! Imagine the chaos he could cause!"

The cat nodded and leapt back down in one bound, landing on the back of a small sofa. Eliza helped him remove a spiderweb from his whiskers. "The question that remains is, what do we do about it?" asked Pal.

"Okay, so we know Professor Kent will likely be busy working with Principal Crinwere all night and they plan to carry out their plan tomorrow during the school day," said Eliza. "Do we intercept? Do we warn Faye? Do we try to warn the principal? Do we let them take her stuff, and *then* try to prevent Professor Kent having any access to the information he's looking for?"

The cat pondered for a moment. "Professor Kent is after the book Faye kept her notes in. It would be small enough to take it without drawing too much attention. I think it's better not to try to go after Kent's reputation. It could quickly turn ugly. Accusing someone often backfires."

"Even with his diary as proof?" probed Eliza.

"His diary is proof that he wants to take away people's magic. Faye has been taking people's souls. It looks like the magic leaving them is a side-effect. Remember when she said trauma could cause someone to lose their magic? The way you described those souls in the mirror, they sound traumatized to me. I don't think Professor Kent could be very interested in taking people's souls, and this diary would only prove his innocence."

"Fine." Eliza kicked the edge of the desk and regretted it instantly when the pain surged into her big toe. Gritting her teeth, she continued, "We just have to get the book stealthily and destroy it?"

The cat was so still Eliza waved her hand in front of its face, "I'm thinking," Pal said irritably. "We can't destroy it until we're sure all the victims' souls are returned to their mortal bodies. Getting the book might be easy enough, but we shouldn't be in a hurry to destroy it."

"Okay. We could get to Faye's room first thing in the morning and take the book of shadows," said Eliza.

Pal agreed, "That way Professor Kent never gets hold of it. The principal reverses the curses with Faye's help. She'll have taken the potion to cooperate, so they won't need the book, and everyone who lost their soul gets it back. You become a hero for saving the school!" declared the cat, purring loudly.

"It sounds easy... I guess there's nothing to it but to go to bed and hope things go as planned in the morning."

Pal stretched fully on the back of the sofa, blinking slowly as he did so. "Bed sounds like a fantastic idea. I think I've been awake a full four hours without a nap. One could accuse you of cruelty for not letting me sleep!"

"Yeah, yeah," said Eliza, holding out an arm so the cat could leap onto it. She walked out of the office and slowly made her way through a tunnel that led toward her dorm room, cradling Pal in her arms. He was so deeply asleep when they reached her room that she just laid him gently on the bed and slid under the covers next to him.

"Goodnight, Pal," she whispered to him, gently stroking the bridge of his nose. He slept on.

CHAPTER FIFTEEN

Confrontation

I am a self-sabotaging idiot. That's what Eliza told herself as she woke up forty-five minutes late for her first class, having slept through breakfast.

"To be fair, we had a late night!" Pal called out as he trotted alongside her. Eliza was running up the steps two at a time to get to Faye's dorm room.

"Yes, but now we have no idea whether—" but Eliza slid to a halt as she reached the hall. The Necromancy and Herbalism professors were already there, standing in the doorway teleporting the contents of Faye's room to a new location.

"Hey!" called Eliza, "where are you sending that stuff?"

Professor Claeg sneered at her, "I would not divulge such sensitive information to a student."

Eliza banged her fist against the wall, frustrated, and clutched a stitch in her side. Professor Walker touched her arm kindly and said "Run along to your class, dear. And remember to act as though you suspect nothing."

This took Eliza aback. She had not expected that Principal Crinwere would have told staff of her involvement. Recovering, it occurred to Eliza to feel the injustice of being excluded from the conclusion of a mystery that had marked her first year at Kentree. The likelihood that Eliza would be remembered as having played any important role in the whole ordeal was becoming more obscure.

She turned and jogged toward her class. From the third story hall she knew she could go into the North-East tower and use the covered bridge to cross the buildings and get to her classroom faster. Coming to a halt outside Transposition, Eliza caught her breath for a moment before making her way into the classroom. She tried to cross to her seat without drawing any attention to herself.

Unfortunately, her timing was terrible. Students all began to conjure exactly as Eliza made to run across the front of the class toward her usual seat. When she was precisely in the middle of the classroom, cries erupted from all sides and she was promptly covered in every shade of sticky, warm goo—some students conjured what smelled of bubble gum and others a smell horribly like sewage. All the streams collided in the middle exactly where Eliza had just launched herself and she was taken under by the impact.

Her whole body was submerged in the stuff. She could not breathe, and the viscosity was so dense she could barely move her arms. She tried not to open her mouth to scream in panic, but the goo was making its way up her nostrils. She felt bile coming up her esophagus, making her want to retch at the sensation.

Just then, all the goo dissolved and Professor Neach remained standing in the middle of the room, wand aloft. "What do you think you're doing, stupid woman! You could have gotten yourself killed! Go sit in your seat and try to catch up, will you!" Eliza stumbled to her seat, feeling horrible and humiliated. She heard Professor Neach continue to insult her tardiness and stupidity as she sat down and pulled the day's worksheet toward her.

Eliza did not pay any attention in class, she could not think under what circumstance conjuring goo could possibly be useful. She worried that she was missing her opportunity to thwart Professor Kent from getting access to the information he needed to become a magical tyrant. In the end she was assigned extra homework because all she had succeeded in expelling from her wand was a small squirt of what looked disgustingly like mucus.

She hurried to the Grand Room for lunch, now starving and highly anxious, and was shocked to see Faye sitting at the lunch table, helping herself to fruit and vegetables. Mashu sat next to her digging into a soup, oblivious to anything suspicious. Melissa had not returned to sit with them since the day Mashu's claw had been taken.

Eliza glimpsed Melissa sneaking out of the hall through another doorway with a crudely made sandwich in her hands. Melissa did not look disheveled today. Her blonde hair was braided in a warrior braid on the top of her head, and she had used eye liner to draw runes onto her hands and face. It might have looked ridiculous to someone else, but Eliza knew Melissa had unlocked new ways to bring out what little magic remained in her. When Eliza looked back at her usual table, she noticed Faye's dark eyes had also been watching Melissa leaving the hall. Eliza approached the round table and sat across from Faye.

"There you are," said Faye. "Why weren't you here at breakfast?"

"I overslept," replied Eliza, serving herself soup and several rolls of bread. "Did I miss anything?"

"No, but I told Mashu about your wand going missing. How was your magic this morning?" Faye's tone was indifferent, but Mashu looked at Eliza with interest.

"Wha—? Yes, my wand is missing. I wasn't very good in class this morning, but it might be because I was distracted and arrived halfway through the lesson…" Eliza held her hand over the bowl of soup and concentrated on extracting the heat.

With a dull crack, the surface of the soup froze solid. Eliza now focused on directing heat through her hand and warming the soup, which reached a simmering boil a few seconds later. "Looks like I've still got it!" Eliza tried to sound relieved, but she was too preoccupied about the next phase of Principal Crinwere and Professor Kent's plan.

Faye nodded, looking into Eliza's eyes. The former was in deep concentration and the latter started when Faye's voice rang clearly inside her head. *I know what you've done.*

Eliza jumped so violently she spilled Mashu's orange juice all over the table. "What?!" she said out loud.

But Faye was already getting up, "I'll see you guys later," she said and floated unhurriedly out of the hall.

Mashu cleaned up the mess of juice with a wave of his wand and looked at Eliza, "If we've been targeted as the next victims of the magic thief, Faye's probably next. They might be waiting for a certain star alignment. We still don't know how the magic works. They could be planning on taking all three of us down at once."

Distracted, Eliza said something vague in agreement. Faye was supposed to have been detained in her morning class. She wasn't sure if she should tell Mashu what had transpired, either about Melissa or Faye. She chewed her lip in preoccupation.

Mashu scratched the side of his hairy face, "We should talk to Melissa again. She's been researching day and night. She might have some stuff to try but needs more, well, magic to set it into motion."

Again, Eliza's reply was in agreement though she hardly knew what she was agreeing to. The memory of Faye's voice echoed inside her head. *I know what you've done,* she said. Why was Faye still attending classes and meals as if nothing had occurred? What was she planning? Should she not be on the run at this very moment? Anxiety ate at Eliza while she tried to settle on what she ought to do.

Should she try to speak to Principal Crinwere again? Talk to Melissa, who spent these past months desperately trying to uncover the truth? Find Faye and try to convince her of the error of her ways? Wildly, Eliza even considered going to confront Professor Kent but dismissed this option quickly. He was not the villain today, and she could hardly pull him out of the probable confrontation with Faye in order to fulfil her desire to feel like she was doing *something.* For all she knew, Professor Kent's proficiency with Sorcery could be the deciding factor should the confrontation become violent.

Eliza had just decided on the unfulfilling option

that she ought to study for her exams and hope that the faculty sorted everything out. It was by no means a satisfactory solution, but it was what she had been explicitly told to do. This decision was also exacerbated by Eliza's inability to conceive of any way she could make herself useful in taking down the threat that had been her trusted friend at Kentree.

Eliza used Transposition to pull a wooden staff from her room that she had been working on in Energy Amplification. She prepared to work on the staff studiously all afternoon. To her immense relief, she was saved from this dull fate when the entire school shuddered as if an earthquake had hit the building.

Springing to action at last, Eliza and Mashu locked eyes for just a second before abandoning all their things at the table and lurching sideways off their seats. They bolted to the door. The school shook again and Eliza stumbled into a few students who darted past her. She glanced up at the hall's ceiling which she knew to be held up only by spell work and decided to take a precautionary measure. She closed her eyes and guided a protective dome to suspend itself below the magical repair and felt reassured that at the very least should a stone come loose, her additional spell would protect anyone below.

There was chaos when they reached the hallway. Students were running out the front doors. Others cowered in corners. There was much confusion as bodies ran out of classrooms, or else dashed into them. There were some loud screams as another shudder shook the ground and the mass of students who had just been pushing to leave from the back doors were now creating a solid wall as they came running back inside, away from whatever threat they had witnessed out back.

Eliza and Mashu were crushed against a wall by the sudden rush of pupils pushing to head out the front gates. Eliza grasped Mashu's shoulder, she could just reach him with her arm outstretched, and called "The back courtyard!"

Mashu threw a thick hairy arm around Eliza and threw her into a piggyback position on his strong back. He ran through the swarm of panicked students. Arms wrapped firmly around Mashu's shoulders, Eliza saw Melissa appear from a hallway that led to the dorms and called to her, "Sweet! Outside! Now!" Melissa nodded. She carried a huge and colourful staff ready in her hands and started forcing her way through the crowd. Mashu was quicker and soon Melissa was lost from view.

Mashu was wide and his short, stocky legs carried him securely. Though the crowd attempted to push through them, he did not trip, fall, or let himself get jostled off course. He gathered momentum and soon students were throwing themselves into the walls to let him pass. Eliza clung onto his broad shoulders without elegance.

They burst outside into the courtyard, into what was becoming a warm spring day. The snow had melted, leaving soggy brown grass beneath the afternoon sun. Birds sang cheerfully unaware of anything strange occurring below them. Only a few panicked students remained in the courtyard; they ran through the manicured garden toward the forest, looking for cover.

Mashu and Eliza were struck by a tremendous beauty floating ten feet above the stone patio of the courtyard. It wasn't until Mashu gave Eliza a shake that she recalled her position on his back. Sliding down to set her feet upon the stone, she surveyed the scene before her. Faye was suspended in the air. Her arms spread gently on either side of her body, her straight black hair rose elegantly around her as if she were under water.

Emanating from Faye was an electric energy quite unlike any Eliza had ever witnessed in her short time studying magic. Fire and water were the most common ways of expressing magic. Electricity was advanced. The clap of thunder created by the charges of magic was of such strength that the ground trembled. Calm painted Faye's features despite the unusual circumstances. Beneath her were eight professors and the principal, each trying in vain to contain her.

At second glance, Eliza saw Faye's lips were moving slightly. Eliza supposed she must be working a complicated incantation. The spell was just beginning.

"Faye!" growled Mashu in indignation. Quite having forgotten that Mashu knew nothing of Faye's guilt, Eliza was too slow to stop him reacting protectively. He threw himself into the professors and knocked four down as easily as bowling pins. Mashu jumped free of the tangle of limbs and prepared to charge the other professors who were now turning their magic onto him. Eliza saw that Faye's attention had been distracted by Mashu's eruptive interference. She looked at him lovingly.

"I'm sorry I deceived you." Faye's voice rang supernaturally loud as she addressed Mashu. "If I can find a cure for this, we could do anything. We could go anywhere you want."

Mashu gaped at Faye in bewilderment. Before he could understand what was happening, the professors had recovered themselves.

"*Enough!*" cried Principal Crinwere. One hand was held out toward Mashu and a wand was pointed at him with the other. Before Eliza could do more than choke out a startled cry, the principal had teleported Mashu away. Stunned, Eliza looked around for him for a moment before coming to her senses. Of course, he would have been removed to someplace where he would not be able to interfere again.

Faye lost interest at this development and was looking skyward again, chanting something Eliza could not hear. Her voice became part of the wind and mixed itself into various melodies. Eliza felt the hair on the back of her neck stand on end as the air around them became charged with magic. A loud CRACK rent the air with such force the ground beneath their feet shook more violently than ever. Faye was awe inspiring in the greatness of her power. Her eyes pure black and magic pulsing from within her in waves of intense energy. The effect was breathtaking.

The professors were all attempting to contain Faye. Professor Walker had taken to lobbing Scalpere vines up into the air to try to bring Faye down with their razor-sharp needles. Fireballs rained down on Faye and potions bottles smashed at her sides. Professor Kent conjured ropes and chains to try to hold her.

Nothing had any effect. Faye did not notice any of their attacks; nothing managed to touch her. The plants, potions, and spells bounced away from Faye a few inches before making contact with her body. She was in a league of her own, covered by a protective spell stronger than any of the combined attacks the faculty could muster. Eliza closed her eyes in concentration and reached up to Faye with her mind. *What are you doing?*

She felt a stir of recognition.

What I must to gain my freedom.

Eliza reached Faye's mind to let her know that she

understood. *Will you hurt anyone?*

She felt a painful stab in her head and Faye's reply was clear. *Only if anyone stands in my way. What happens when I attempt this spell is a mystery even to me. Eliza, don't try to stop me.*

I won't, was Eliza's improbable promise. *Why could you not do this somewhere remote where no one could get hurt?*

Amusement met this thought, *I am more generous than you think. If the magic goes wrong and puts the world in danger, there is a good chance that someone here will be able to stop it sooner than if it were unleashed somewhere isolated.*

Without warning the connection was broken; Eliza was thrown unceremoniously out of Faye's mind and back into her own. She stumbled a little at the abrupt break in connection and looked up again. The air around the courtyard was turning a hazy reddish colour and the sky continued to rumble as though by thunder. Eliza reached her magic down into the earth and asked the ground beneath the school to stand firm in the face of the tremors that occurred around them. The earth outside of the school could absorb all the shocks, but the ground below the walls *must stand firm. Please*.

Returning her mind into her body, Eliza examined how else she could mitigate destruction, but things were starting to look freaky. The air surrounding Faye was being ripped apart, the very fabric of reality wearing away. Through this shredded veil, other worlds, other landscapes, were now visible. With a shock, Eliza realized that more was coming from these windows than mere images. A burst of wind devoid of oxygen and colder than any winter winds she had ever known knocked her down onto her backside and left her seeing stars.

The red haze Eliza had seen accumulating around the scene was crimson sand. It was filling the air around them so densely they struggled to see. It was coming from another of these ragged windows. About to cast heat to protect herself from the frozen blast of air, Eliza was detained by a hot rush which came spilling out from a different tear; with it came a strong whiff of methane. Eliza pulled her wand from her belt and cast a protective spell toward the gateways and tried to block the immense heat from crossing into their world.

A piercing scream from the other side of the circle drew everyone's eyes. Derren Angel, professor of Empathology and Mentalism, was being rained on from a fresh portal some twelve meters from where Eliza stood. The rain fell horizontally and covered him in clear liquid that quickly began to harden on impact. His strangled cry of pain carried around the grounds despite the thunder and wind; goosebumps rose on Eliza's skin at the sight of the man becoming overwhelmed.

"Liquid glass!" yelled Professor Stone who reached Professor Angel's side first. He was wearing several talismans around his neck and drew a wand from his holster. He crossed the wand over his staff in the shape of an X and began calling upon his magic to contain the horror of the glass rain. More teachers had reached the scene, and everyone was doing what they could to fight the foreign elements.

With everyone aiming their magic at preventing the mysteries that could come lurching into their world through these shredded veils, there was no one left to distract Faye. Only Faye remained uninterested in the chaos unfolding around her. She continued to float serenely above them, creating more and more doorways in the fabric of what Eliza quickly determined to be Reality, unleashing further Unrealities into their safe, precious little world.

"*STOP*!" Eliza shouted at Faye. "Can't you see what you're doing?"

But Faye did not respond, did not look down, did not hesitate in the spell she continued to cast. The shouts of the teachers rang in Eliza's ears. She became aware that some students were beginning to appear around the outer edges of the courtyard, timidly offering a helping hand in an impossible battle.

Rage pounded in Eliza's ears. Rage so powerful she

felt her nose prickle with the injustice of it. How could someone be so singularly self-involved that they would risk their entire universe collapsing? Just so she could be a little more solid, a little more in control? How bad could flickering between two worlds really be, that she would go to such lengths and risk killing thousands of species just to get what she wanted? It was absurd, thought Eliza; it would have been better to choose death than to choose one's own life at the risk of so many others.

Eliza's fingers closed over a crystal that she carried in her pocket. It was a large, six-sided clear quartz crystal onto which she had carved her favourite rune. Eliza closed her eyes, the crystal clutched in one hand and her wand held in the other hand. But she did not cast any incantations, did not attempt to recite any spells. Casting goo and transporting objects, creating fireballs or fountains was of little use to her today.

Eliza reverted to her most natural form of magic. The magic she had begun to understand even before being admitted to study at Kentree. There was nothing sophisticated or precise about it, and it had only earned her ridicule from Professor Kent. But it was hers.

Communicating directly with the elements, Eliza felt at home again. Not trying to create, contain, or contort as they were taught in Elemental Magic. The tools in her hands only served to amplify her natural ability to communicate with what already existed, with what already had power greater than any sorcerer could ever produce. The very forces of nature could not help but to listen to her small, determined contact. She felt a weight land heavily on her shoulder and she knew Pal had joined her in the fight. The cat was lending her some of his strength, Eliza was grateful.

At first, the many elements whirling around them were too confusing. Eliza could not focus on any one long enough to communicate or understand. The energies were foreign, the chemical make-up so unusual Eliza could make neither heads nor tails of any of it. Stones spat through a rip and battered her and Pal so painfully they were forced to retreat a few feet back, letting Professor Walker take the lead on casting a net of vines to contain the pelting rocks.

Eliza stumbled backward and fell to one knee. She could barely open her eyes; the air was too full of vile contaminants and sand being churned around by savage winds. Coughing, Eliza held Pal with one arm and continued her retreat. It was no use. She could barely see anything despite the day having been perfectly clear. It was dark even though it couldn't be past two in the afternoon.

She tripped on something and her chin collided with something hard on the ground. A volcanic rock that must have been expelled from one of the many open gateways. She scraped her elbows when landing, trying to protect Pal from the force of the fall. The flat stone of the courtyard was no longer visible. She dug her fingers into the red sand that now covered the earth and felt the stone an inch or so below.

"When the going gets tough, the tough get going," came a cheerful voice. Squinting up, Eliza saw Melissa Sweet beaming down at her, extending a helping hand. Eliza took it, grinning, and allowed herself to be pulled up.

"I can always trust you to think of something positive to say," Eliza said, and Melissa laughed merrily. It was as if they were back in class, discussing the latest assignment.

"How about this weather we're having?" asked Melissa, having to shout over the wind. "It seems to me I remember a certain witch who excels at this type of magic. You were having a go at it already, weren't you?"

Eliza coughed in the dust storm, "I was but I can't concentrate while being attacked from all sides."

Melissa, holding a huge ornately decorated staff, merely smiled. The staff was incomprehensibly complex. Made of at least seven different species of wood, tens of crystals, with runes carved into every inch of the staff, and, to complete the strangeness of the object, there were a few bags of herbs tied along the length of it. Melissa said she could protect Eliza. She placed a hand on Eliza's shoulder and concentrated on the task with both eyes shut. It was nothing to what Melissa would have been able to do with her abilities intact, but there was a distinct drop in the wind and particles of sand that came scratching at Eliza's face and throat. Melissa had created a magical instrument so potently capable of amplifying magic, that what little magic she had left was strong enough for this. Melissa, with her unabashed optimism, created a magic so pure, clean, and good that Eliza's spirits were quite recovered.

Encouraged by Melissa's determined inability to give up, Eliza returned to work with Pal on her shoulder. She felt her way into the foreign energies coming from each gateway. She greeted each strangeness and invited them to return to their Reality. Some were receptive to this suggestion, but more were quite unable to acquiesce as the tides behind them pushed too strongly forward to go back. To them, Eliza suggested they direct their damaging effects onto the agent of their removal from their own world.

For the first time Faye let out a gasp of surprise. A chilling breeze blew across her from one of the portals. Crying aloud in pain, pellets shot at Faye from another gateway. A strong wind began to spin and disorient her. No longer a mask of calm, floating above the scene, Faye was now being pulled into the fight by her own weapons. Eliza did not stop. She started peeling off the protective spells she and the professors had cast, and allowed every terror which had been held back to be unleashed. With her guidance, they directed themselves at Faye.

Having almost finished separating herself from the other world, Faye did not relinquish so easily. She continued with her incantation, yelling strange words as she became consumed by freezing cold from one side, and hot magma from another. Only when the molten glass rain began to fill her mouth was the spell detained. Soon, nothing was left floating over the scene but what appeared to be an overlarge silver cocoon. Faye was encased entirely within.

Eliza did not open her eyes to see any of this. She knew it was happening just as she knew that the professors had all stopped their assaults on the doorways to locate the cause of the new development. Eliza did not give herself a moment to feel satisfaction. She knew she was not capable of a magic to match Faye's, but she knew she could guide natural elements to do the work that needed to be done. Pal's tail was wrapped around her neck, and she began analyzing the different energies available and encouraged them to mix in such a way that would allow the tears in Reality to heal themselves.

There was no way Eliza could understand the magic that had caused the portals, but she realized she didn't need to understand. Nature understood itself, and where a force was capable of destruction, it was also capable of healing. Eliza asked the torn fabric of her world whether it knew how to heal itself and invited it to do so. She lent it whatever energies it needed to make itself whole again. One by one the portals began to close until the wind had died down and the world was stable. Finally, quiet filled the air. There was a small cough from someone nearby. A pained groan came from further away.

Eliza opened her eyes to assess the scene. All the gateways were closed. The professors were scattered, bruised and bleeding, but quickly coming to their sense of responsibility. They picked themselves up from the rubble and began helping those who had been wounded. In the middle of all this destruction was the glass cocoon suspended only a few feet above the ground. Eliza looked at it curiously, she could feel Faye was still inside, but she felt something had changed about her friend. She walked up to the glass and placed a hand upon it. The surface was rough but cool to the touch. She pressed her forehead upon it and laid both palms flat on the surface.

"Are you sure you want to let her out?" asked Pal.

Eliza smiled, "I don't think she'll be a threat to anyone anymore."

She gave the cocoon a gentle push and it fell to the flagstone patio and shattered. Inside retched and sputtered a woman so unlike Faye that Eliza felt she was seeing Faye for the first time. A version of Faye stripped of glamour. A Faye who was capable of harvesting innocent people's souls in search of a cure. A Faye who did not care if universes collapsed. Not as long as she could be whole. The real Faye.

"You did it," said Eliza coldly. "You freed yourself of your curse."

CHAPTER SIXTEEN

Balance Restored

Trembling, Faye tried to rise. She got slowly onto her hands and knees, and then raised herself painfully to her feet. Faye *did* have wings; Eliza could finally see them. But something was wrong with them. They were not shimmering like jewels the way faeries' wings would. Faye's wings were charcoal grey dappled with black. They were peeling horribly, large scaly flakes falling away.

Her face was much altered, too. No longer could she pass for twenty. The face belonged to a woman in her sixties, and the hair that had been so boldly black mere minutes before was now streaked with gray. Faye turned to look at her wings and her horror showed clearly on her face. She touched the edge of one with delicate fingers and it dissolved into her hand.

"You're a normal woman now," said Eliza. "Bound only to this world," Eliza was certain this had never been part of Faye's plan. "A Mundunce."

Faye looked nauseated. "This—this cannot be all I get. I've pushed the boundaries of magic, how can I be stripped of everything I am? I perfected the spell! The last few people—I separated the soul and the magic and put it back, they didn't even feel a thing—I perfected it!" She looked wretched and desperate.

Eliza looked sheepishly to one side, "That's a little bit my fault. The portals were hungry for energy and I wouldn't have had nearly enough to close them all myself." Eliza could not suppress a guilty smile that played upon her lips, "I might have directed them to help themselves to your power in order to heal themselves shut again."

Faye looked fragile as tears welled up in her eyes. She looked so pitiful that Eliza nearly regretted her interference. She could tell her old friend was tired, and Eliza used Transposition to bring forth a chair from the Grand Room to the courtyard and directed Faye to sit upon it. Too drained to argue, Faye acquiesced in an instant and sat her tired bones gratefully down into the chair. She nodded quickly to sleep, perched uncomfortably in the seat.

Silence settled like dust upon the scene. Some moans issued from Holly Quaker who was being revived after having been overwhelmed by a discharge from one of the portals. Eliza scratched Pal on the head, just to give herself something to do. Together they observed the moment in silence, unsure what should happen next.

Professor Kent and Principal Crinwere finally extricated themselves from the others, once it was assured that all injured parties were in the safe hands of Nepi Teget, Professor of Healing. Healing students rushed to the scene as well, to assist. On approaching Faye, Professor Kent and Principal Crinwere looked grim.

"Well, it looks like Faye got what she wanted," said Principal Crinwere glumly, a few small cuts played across their forehead. "No more need to apply to me for any more access to our private archives! She hasn't got a drop of magic left in her."

"I wonder why she decided to rip the world apart. It doesn't make sense," Eliza mused.

"From what we recovered in her room this morning, it looks like Faye was experimenting with prohibited magic. Taking tokens from her victims to practice what splitting their essence could do to them. She was never trying to take their magic to make herself more powerful, she was testing whether it was possible. With the other half of her soul in another reality, she had to break open the barriers between those universes. I think she wanted to emerge whole on this side. She was to open the doorway, split herself, bring the other half that was trapped in the other world to this one, and then reunite the two pieces. Why there were so many open doorways… possibly as a distraction? More likely Faye hadn't had the chance to perfect that magic," Principal Crinwere mused, "The fabric of reality is fragile. Pull one thread, the rest unravels."

All were silent, watching the faery wings on Faye's back continue to dissolve.

"But what about the people whose magic she took?" interjected Eliza. "Will you be able to restore the souls that were taken?"

Principal Crinwere answered delicately. Melissa Sweet stood close by, ears strained to hear the answer. "Yes, it is likely we will. I believe Faye had discovered how to reunite the soul and magic with the body a few weeks ago. That's why she was finally able to perform her spell. She knew she could separate herself and restore herself fully in just one world."

"I don't understand why she's frail now," wondered Professor Kent. "I would have thought she should be all powerful once her two halves were reunited."

"That's my bad," said Eliza. "She would have come out whole on this side if I hadn't used her magic to close the doorways," she explained. "Her spell worked; she was fully in this world. But I needed to close those portals. More magic was needed to do that than even she had accumulated in her decades of practice. She was drained of every drop."

Principal Crinwere and Professor Kent both looked impressed by this piece of information. The three fell into a contemplative silence broken only when Melissa Sweet spoke.

"Everyone who lost their magic has their soul and magic preserved somewhere, then? We can reunite them?"

"Have patience," said Principal Crinwere. "We should be able to, but it may take some time. I believe Professor Claeg will be the most familiar with the magic required. He will be studying all the material Miss Griggs had before he jumps in and rashly tries reversing any curses."

Melissa nodded, barely masking her disappointment.

Eliza's eyes flickered uneasily between Professor Kent and Principal Crinwere. "Could someone use this magic to take people's power? People who they think shouldn't have it, or to punish people who use magic for evil?"

A shadow played across Professor Kent's face. "Any magic that disturbs the soul of the victim, also disrupts the soul of the person conjuring. No doubt at first Faye did not realize that was what she was doing. She did not realize that what she was taking were souls. The act of taking a soul from a victim is of a most perverse evil. She was becoming more cursed with each instance that she used this magic. Dark magic does not serve a master; it only curses them."

"—she used to be the life of this place!" exclaimed

Principal Crinwere, "Everyone wanted to be friends with her. She made everyone laugh and helped everyone around her when they needed it —"

"—then around the end of last year, there was a shift," said Professor Brown, stepping forward. "We all noticed it but thought it was because her fourth study proposal was rejected. We knew she wanted to solve her problem, and assumed she was becoming so focused that she was letting friendships fall aside."

The frail Faye mumbled in her sleep, still seated awkwardly. Eliza looked at Principal Crinwere and Professor Kent, "Did you think she could be the one taking magic all along, then?"

"Not at all!" exclaimed Principal Crinwere. "The idea that such a lovely girl would begin cruel experimentation on students was beyond my imagination. I assure you; she was very well liked among the staff and students."

Professor Kent said, "It was only this morning that we understood what had really changed. Faye started her experiments on magical creatures before moving onto students. She captured pixies, sprites, and faeries in the woods here. She started experimenting with them before progressing to humans. From her diary we were able to learn that some of the earliest experiments died from the shock of having their souls ripped away. She was very disturbed by the results, especially as her own father is a faery. She felt the sting of murder. But the shadow of dark magic had already taken its hold, and the experimentation did not end there. She discovered after a few failed experiments that the subjects were more likely to survive if that essence that she was harvesting was preserved in a vessel. That's why you saw a collection of souls in that mirror. It helps the victims live even though they've been terribly altered."

Eliza felt goosebumps, imagining Faye's initial anguish at taking a creature's life. She imagined the dark magic casting a shadow on Faye's soul, compelling her to continue. Faye became unable to stop. Obsessed. Corrupted.

"Considering how much it warps the person who performs this magic, it's unlikely anyone will want to try it for themselves, then," said Eliza, watching Professor Kent's reaction closely.

He knew what she was really asking, and answered plainly, "I cannot think of any cause worth mangling one's own soul. A magic this evil... very unlikely, indeed."

Students had begun creeping toward them from inside the school now that the commotion had passed. The sun was shining on them once again, and all picked their way around the boulders, through pebbles, sand, and broken glass. Mashu pushed through the other students to run to

Faye's fragile figure. He touched her forehead gently with his thumb. A fat tear fell down his cheek. He turned his gaze to Eliza questioningly. She tried to communicate with her eyes that she would explain everything later. Mashu seemed to understand because he turned back to Faye wordlessly and lifted her into his arms.

"I'm going to take her to Professor Teget," he said, and carried Faye carefully toward the Healer. No one stopped him. There was no reason to.

A crowd of students now formed a half-circle around the ruined courtyard and Eliza started to feel self-conscious. She knew she was older than most of the student population, and she was standing apart from them with the professors who, to younger eyes, looked like her peers. She felt peculiarly out of place. She belonged to neither group, and yet she belonged to both. She was a student, *and* she stood with the people who fought to protect the school. It was Professor Brown, of Cooperation with Beings, who broke the silence between the two groups.

"A terrible curse was unleashed here today," she called to the crowd. "And even with the combined force of our faculty, we were no match for it. We were fighting a losing battle."

An expectant hush fell over the crowd, but many eyes were already looking directly at Eliza. Blushing, Eliza had a vision of many students watching the events unfolding with their noses pressed against the stained-glass windows from inside the school. Many had already seen what happened.

Professor Brown continued, "It was our newest student, who joined us a month into the school year and worked many long hours to catch up, who reminded us what magic *is.* Magic is not offensive, nor defensive. As the rest of us were flailing around ineffectually against elements from worlds beyond our own, it was Eliza," Professor Brown stopped next to her and put a hand on her shoulder, "who was the one who used magic for what it is—energy. She did not fight it, she did not resist it, she did not attempt to overcome it. Eliza did what none of us were courageous enough to do. She redirected the energy, allowing it to flow as it wished and using its own momentum to return balance."

Eliza felt her face burning. She wanted to be a celebrated witch, of course, but she felt like an imposter standing there receiving recognition for something she did without really thinking about it. It was an obvious solution. Surely anyone who had thought of it would have done the job just as well as she had.

Professor Brown pressed two fingers to her lips, lifted those two fingers towards Eliza then pressed them against her own heart. The other professors followed suit, using the same gesture. All the students did the same. Pal purred loudly on Eliza's shoulder.

"Thank you, Eliza, for your services to our school," said Professor Brown and clasped Eliza's hand into a firm handshake. The professor made her way back through the crowd toward the school, her long skirt dragging in the red sand. The principal was next to approach Eliza.

"Thank you, Eliza, for your contribution today," Principal Crinwere grasped her hand in a strong handshake and followed Professor Brown into the school.

Each faculty member shook Eliza's hand, except Professor Neach who had been severely injured and was not conscious. Then the students came forth, timidly at first but eventually pushing forward enthusiastically. They all wanted to shake Eliza's hand and give Pal a pat on the head. They had none of the gravitas the professors had. They were charged with awe and enthusiasm. Melissa reappeared in front of Eliza after a few minutes of this, tears of joy streaming from her eyes, and she threw herself heartily into Eliza's arms. Eliza eagerly returned the hug.

"They'll be able to cure us," said Melissa, "Vigilante justice might not have worked, but we got there eventually!"

Eliza nodded energetically at Melissa, "Yes, you'll be cured, I'm sure of it!" Melissa sobbed a laugh and choked a croak-y "Thank you" before rushing through the crowd and up the steps into the school. Eliza had no doubt that she was heading to Professor Claeg's office immediately to offer any help she could.

Eventually, Eliza had been thumped heartily on the back so many times that she was beginning to feel overstimulated. Sparks of electricity began crackling at the tips of her hair and Pal, who had received many pets and ear-scratches, was also beginning to flick his tail in irritation. Politely, Eliza extricated herself from the crowd of admiring students and removed her wand from its holster at her waist. She cast a spell on herself that made it difficult for anyone to focus on her, and darted through the halls until she reached the safety of her dorm.

Eliza and Pal collapsed onto the bed. She looked at him, a perfect shining black cat, and smiled. "You're the best friend I could ever ask for," she said.

Pal curled up into the crook of her arm and together they lay there, quite still, simply existing. After so much tension and adventure, it was good just to decompress. Several people knocked at her door as the hours passed but it could all wait. Right now, Eliza wanted nothing more than to share a few quiet moments with Pal.

The last few weeks of the semester passed in a happy blur. Eliza found herself now fully part of her classmates' social circle. Melissa had marched Eliza to the table of sixteen-year-olds and placed her in the seat of honour in the middle and— like magic—Eliza immediately seemed to belong there. She and Melissa eventually sat in the middle of a series of tables that were pushed together. This became where nearly everyone in her year crowded together to share meals, magical theories, and study.

Despite her initial distaste for being surrounded by so many people, Eliza was beginning to enjoy it. It felt nice to be part of a community. The stimulating conversations of her younger classmates had a buoyant effect on her. They were all just as positive and optimistic about the future as Melissa had always been, and their enthusiasm was refreshing. Eliza began to forget the decade of conforming to society's rat race and began to truly believe that even though she was fast approaching her thirties, anything was still possible for her.

Eliza told Mashu the whole story of what happened one afternoon as they strolled the gardens. Tulips were quickly overtaking daffodils and bees were working their way from stem to stem. Mashu chose to remain faithfully by Faye's side as she recovered in the Healer's room. The two of them left the school together one sunny afternoon, a couple weeks before the end of term.

No one could do anything to help Faye recover her magic. Her soul had become too damaged by the dark magic which corrupted her. Mashu would escort her back to her family. Perhaps in time, she might heal what had been broken. Though Faye did not look at or speak to Eliza, Mashu gave her a smile and a wave goodbye.

It took a few weeks to convince Professor Claeg to start reuniting the severed souls with their bodies. Once he did, Melissa immediately returned to her usual over-achieving, show-off self. But Eliza did not mind. The trees were now fully in their leaves and flowers were blooming in all the school gardens.

It was only a few days before the exams in June that Melissa had her magic back. Eliza and the other first year students worked day and night to help Melissa perfect all the spells she had not been able to perform since before Christmas. Luckily, Melissa had painstakingly memorized the theory these past months. Her success was quick.

Eliza's grade passed all their exams with record-breaking performance. The professors associated it to the teamwork and camaraderie that had sprung up amongst the students in the lead up to exams. Eliza knew it was all down to Melissa, who was now celebrating the end of exams by producing a most impressive multi-colored light show from her staff.

Professor Stone had come to congratulate Melissa on her craftsmanship, and offered to give her one-on-one time in his classroom to refine her instrument. By the end of the semester, Melissa's staff was no longer a huge clunky thing, but a work of art much admired by the rest of the students. The magic Melissa was now able to produce was of exquisite composition, much influenced by the staff's many ingredients.

When the very last day of school finally rolled around and it was time to return home for a two-month break, Eliza found herself standing in front of the principal.

"How was your first year at Kentree?" Principal Crinwere asked.

"Definitely not what I expected," replied Eliza, thinking back to how naively she had imagined herself immediately outperforming the rest of the students, "but I cannot wait to come back for a second year!"

Eliza and Pal braced themselves as Holly Quaker raised her wand. She caught a glimpse of Kent standing by the front doors before she felt Holly's spell hit her. With the familiar sensation of bursting into innumerable pieces, she was teleported home.

Pal and Eliza unlocked the door to her bungalow, the tenant who had rented it for their own school year had left the place looking a little different.

With a few waves of her wand, the furniture was quickly back where Eliza liked it, and the kitchen and bathroom had scrubbed themselves spotless. The garden was another thing. With no one to tame the wilderness all spring, it was an eruption of plants and weeds.

Eliza and Pal went out to the garden shed and prepared to plant some new seeds that Eliza had brought back from school. She had purchased a book from the school's shop before coming home about creating habitat for magical creatures and was eager to get to work.

On her hands and knees, digging into her old garden, Eliza felt at peace. This was the site of her first magical manifestations. She felt even happier when, for the first time since her mother's spell had been lifted from her mind, she sat in her garden and watched a plump gnome pluck a fat, juicy strawberry and eat it with great gusto.

AFTERWORD

Thank you for reading Kentree's Stolen Souls, the first in the Kentree series. If you've read this far, I hope you had a few hours of entertainment from Eliza's story.

The world we live in can be a drag; a long boring, slog. This book's only aim is to provide relief from the monotony and allow you, the reader, to escape into something just a little shinier and more magical than Normal Life. Kentree has a few more stories to tell, and this becomes more likely if you tell your friends and family to read it too! If you can spare a moment to leave a rating and a review, it would be much appreciated.

If you would like to share what you hope to see in the next instalment of the Kentree series, please feel free to email me directly at aliqueiles@gmail.com. I look forward to hearing from you.

-     A. Iles

P.S. A companion book titled Garden for Magic

Creatures will be released September 23rd 2023

Manufactured by Amazon.ca
Bolton, ON

35475771R00159